THE DRIVE

PEOPLE ARE TALKING ABOUT...

BEYOND THE RED HILLS

I appreciated the accuracy of the history in this novel. A glimpse at Mr. Yamaguchi was heart wrenching. Billy's ride with his father was a great addition to this story. I loved how Mercy got her name and the timing of her birth. And I loved that Rachel's voice "was like chocolate milk laced with black rum."

Another 5-star book by Patrick Craig and Murray Pura
—Maria R.

THE DRIVE

Book 1—The Storm Riders Series

Murray Pura & Patrick E. Craig

ELK LAKE PUBLISHING INC

PUBLISHING THE POSITIVE
Plymouth, Massachusetts

COPYRIGHT NOTICE

Cover and Interior Design: Derinda Babcock, Deb Haggerty

Editor(s): Cristel Phelps, Deb Haggerty

PUBLISHED BY: Elk Lake Publishing, Inc., 35 Dogwood Drive, Plymouth, MA 02360, 2022

Library Cataloging Data

Names: Pura, Murray and Craig, Patrick (Murray Pura and Patrick Craig)

The Drive: Storm Riders—Book 1 / Murray Pura and Patrick Craig

206 p. 23cm × 15cm (9in × 6 in.)

ISBN-13: 978-1-64949-542-6 (paperback) | 978-1-64949-543-3 (trade paperback) | 978-1-64949-544-0 (e-book)

Key Words: Western, cowboys, cattle drives, romance, outlaws, post-Civil War era, women of the West

Library of Congress Control Number: 2022936573 Fiction

DEDICATION

MURRAY PURA

To the creators and sustainers of that great American literary genre, the western.

PATRICK E. CRAIG

I would like to dedicate this book to Zane Grey, who, from the first time I read Betty Zane at twelve years of age, captured my mind and heart with the spirit of adventure. And, as I grew older and read the sixty or so other novels by him, I also discovered Grey was one of the best romance writers ever to set pen to paper. I hope you find some of both in this book.

ACKNOWLEDGMENTS

MURRAY PURA

I'm grateful to Pat for taking me along on so many literary adventures like this one. It's an enormous blessing to me.

PATRICK E. CRAIG

I would like to acknowledge my coauthor, Murray Pura, for rekindling a spirit of adventure in me through our projects together, and also, for helping keep the Guadalcanal battle scenes in my first Amish novel, without which intervention, that novel would have been meaningless, and this book would not have been written

CHAPTER ONE

PARTNERS

Carson Budrow sat low in the saddle, his slicker doing little to ward off the chill wind and light drops of rain. Far off in the west, over the Staked Plains, random bolts of lightning cut through the growing darkness, and the bitter wind picked up, sending tumbleweeds scooting back along the trail he had just come down. He patted the neck of his horse.

"Well, Ranger, looks like we need to get us a place to spend the night. The storm's headed this way, and we don't want to be out in it when it hits."

The horse jerked his head to the right. Budrow had learned to follow the horse's instincts, and that reliance had carried him safely from Gettysburg all the way to Atlanta with Sherman.

"See something, partner?"

He gave the big black his head and Ranger turned to the right, following a streambed that had intersected their path. About a hundred yards off the trail, they came to a place where the stream had deeply undercut the bank coming around a wide looping turn. There was plenty of room back under the cut for Budrow and his horse. Budrow shook his head. "How on God's green earth do you do that, horse?"

Budrow rode in under the overhang and dismounted slowly. His legs were stiff and his back sore. They had come many miles that day. Budrow pulled the saddle off and rubbed the horse dry with the blanket. Then he poured out a few of the remaining oats before looking around for some wood to build a fire. The horse looked at him mournfully.

"Yeah, yeah, I know, pretty slim pickins. Well, my belly is so empty my throat feels like it got cut. Wait until you see what I have to eat. You'll be grateful."

Budrow could see the storm coming in, and it looked like it would be a howler. Lightning lit the sky, and the horse shifted from foot to foot as the wind picked up some more. He looked around and saw a jam of wood that had swept down the creek, probably during last winter's rains, and piled up in the cut's corner. There was plenty there for a good fire, and soon, he was sitting before a nice blaze. He looked through his saddlebags until he found the last pieces of dried meat. He showed them to the horse, who snorted and stamped his foot.

"I know. Well, we are not eating with the general staff anymore, big fella, so when this storm breaks, we'll try to find a ranch where we can work for some food."

Budrow settled back and stared into the fire. The hot coals glowed red and gold and warmed his tired body. He took off his hat and rubbed his hands through his hair. A flash of lightning lit the sky to the west, and the first heavy drops of rain beat down outside their shelter. The booms of thunder followed the flashes—booming, roaring—like the ranks of cannon booming as they poured ball and shot down into that long line of grey coming out of the trees, across the valley, and up Cemetery Ridge. The grey line kept coming, thinner now, great gaps torn out as blasts of metal chains mixed with shot swept away a hundred men at a time. The Confederate battle flags waving proudly before the men in gray, going down here and there as the men were cut down, some snatched up but most lying on the bloody ground. Now the ranks were thinner. Over the road they came, then the rock wall, and now just a few pushing to the rock wall.

"Gotta hand it to those Rebs, Ranger. They weren't afraid. They died like men."

His eyes went back to the fire, but this time he saw a face, a beautiful face framed by long black hair, the eyes wide and frightened, the dress torn ...

The horse gave a small snort, and his ears flicked forward toward the dark. Budrow quickly turned away from the fire and looked out into the darkness. He sat still for a long moment and then he heard it—a metal shod hoof ringing off a rock. He reached down and unsnapped the holster of his Army Colt. From out of the darkness came a voice.

"Hello, the fire. Can I ride in?"

"Come slow, stranger, let me see all of you before you get down."

The sound of hooves grew louder and then a man riding a big bay horse rode into the circle of light from the fire.

"Howdy, stranger. Can I sit a spell? It's wet out here, and I sure would enjoy that fire. I got some coffee."

"Come on in but come slow."

"Okay, don't get your dander up. I'm just a poor rider out in the wet."

The man climbed down slowly and turned toward the fire. He was dark, mean looking, with a nasty scar down his right cheek. Matted black hair hung down around his face and when he grinned, a front tooth was missing.

Budrow stood up, his hand on the butt of his pistol. "Come in and sit down, but just remember to keep your hands where I can see them."

"Sure, sure, mister." The man grinned again, but there was nothing friendly in it. He reached toward his saddlebag, and Budrow stiffened. Ranger's ears went up. The man stopped and turned his head toward Budrow. "Jest getting out some coffee."

Budrow relaxed, but Ranger didn't.

"Say, where'd you get them nice Yankee pants, pardner? You steal them off a dead bluebelly?"

"Where I get my pants is hardly any of your concern, stranger. But I didn't get them on Saville Row."

"Say-veal? Never heard of that. Say you ain't a Yankee, are you? Texas ain't exactly the place for a Yankee to be wanderin' around, especially mounted on a fine horse like that black."

Budrow's hand slipped down to his pistol, but before he could pull it, he heard a rifle lever clicking in the darkness.

"Wouldn't pull that hawgleg iffin' I was you, Yankee." The voice was followed by a man walking out of the brush, his Winchester pointed straight at Budrow. From the other side of the fire, another man walked in, revolver in his hand.

The scar-faced man grinned again. "Guess I forgot to mention my friends would like to warm themselves too. But now as we are all here, there ain't quite enough room for all of us to fit into this here cave." He pulled his revolver.

The third man tossed a rope he was carrying down in front of Budrow. "He's a Yankee, ain't he? He don't deserve a quick death. He needs to hang up on yonder tree as buzzard bait."

Scarface nodded. "Right as always, Willie. Turn around, Yank."

Budrow turned around. Scarface quickly tied Budrow's hands behind his back.

"Now get over here under this tree." The black-haired stranger quickly made a loop and threw it over Budrow's head. Then he tossed the end over the branch.

"Willie, Jim, put him up on the horse." The two men hoisted Budrow into the saddle as Scarface tied the rope around the tree. He turned back to the horse and raised his hand. "Well, so long, Yank. See you in hell."

Before Scarface could slap the horse's rump, a quiet voice spoke from the darkness. "Ragland, you make a move toward that horse, and I'll shoot your hand off."

Scarface whirled as another man stepped into the light. He wore a leather fringe coat and a shapeless hat, his outfit finished off with the gray trousers of a Rebel soldier. A handlebar mustache hid his mouth, but Budrow could see that his eyes were steel grey. Two shiny Colt revolvers were in his hands. "Drop those guns, boys."

Scarface gasped. "Granite, Granite Roads. What the hell?"

The man spoke quietly, but there was fire underneath. "What are you doing with this man, besides stealing his horse, Ragland?"

"Well, Granite, he's a Yankee."

Granite smiled a wintry smile. "Didn't you hear, boys? The war is over. We lost."

"But he's a Yankee, Granite. We should hang him."

"This will not do, gentleman. Lee surrendered. Lee is a man of honor and so are all his troops. I am a Texan, so honor is doubly important to me. You will not sully our flag by this act. Cut him down."

The man called Willie sneered. "Or what, Corporal Roads?"

"Why, sir, isn't that plain? I will cut you down."

Ragland looked at his friends. There was fear on his face. "Do as he says, Willie, he ain't bluffin'."

Willie and Jim pulled Budrow off the horse. Willie started to pick up his Winchester.

"Leave it lay, Willie." Budrow noticed that even when his benefactor spoke quietly, there was steel and authority in his voice. He put the two revolvers into their holsters. Budrow noticed the holsters were tied down.

"Now, I would suggest you gentlemen, and I use the term loosely since I know you to be cowards, renegades, and scum-sucking desperadoes, I would suggest you mount up and ride. I will not be so hospitable the next time we meet, so I wouldn't look back."

"Sure, Granite, sure." Ragland turned as if to get on his horse and then whirled, pulling his gun as he turned. 'Quicker than lightning' was how Budrow remembered the man called Granite's draw. The right-hand gun roared before Ragland's pistol had even cleared the holster and his gun flew away as Ragland screamed and dropped to his knees, clutching his suddenly bloody fingers. "You shot off my hand, Roads, you shot off my hand."

"I warned you, Ragland. Now it looks like you'll have to learn to shoot left-handed. You two," he motioned toward Willie and Jim, "take yore pard and git!"

Ragland's men boosted the scar-faced man up on his horse. He looked at the man called Granite, pure hate on his face. "If I ever see you again, Granite ..."

"I would suggest, friend Ragland, that seeing me again would be very disadvantageous for your health." The barrel of the long Colt rose to the level of Ragland's belly. "Now clear out."

Ragland cursed and swung his horse. The other two followed him as they clattered away down the creek-bed.

Budrow rubbed his neck where the rope had chafed. "Thank you, sir. I owe you my life. I'm in your debt."

"Think nothing of it, sir. I would do the same for any man I deemed to be at an unfair advantage."

"Carson, Carson Budrow, but my friends call me Kit."

The steel eyes met Budrow's, and there was just a hint of a smile on the chiseled face. "I ain't yore friend, Budrow."

The man called Granite walked into the darkness beyond the fire and returned with a handsome sorrel. The two horses grunted and nickered at each other.

Budrow looked his companion over. "I take it you knew those men?"

"The three of them were under my command at Sharpsburg."

"Your command? I thought they called you corporal?"

"Back then I was a lieutenant." He did not go any further. "What were you in the war?"

"I was a captain in the 18th Pennsylvania Cavalry Regiment. My first action was at Gettysburg."

Roads looked him over. "Was you at Little Round Top? I was there with Hood at Devil's Den."

"Nope, they held us back in Reserve, and I didn't get into that fight. I heard you Texas boys put up a heck of a fine tussle."

Roads nodded. "That we did, son, that we did."

The two men sat silent for a while. Then Roads spoke. "Where you headed, Budrow?"

"West. Maybe California. I don't know. To be honest, I've been on the run since they drummed me out of the Army."

"What was you drummed out for?"

"I shot two of my men who were trying to rape a plantation owner's daughter. The one who got away made out that I was the rapist. They were going to hang me, but I broke out and got away."

Roads looked Budrow over. "You gave up your career to defend a woman?"

"Yes, sir, I did. Her honor was at stake. I could do no less."

Roads looked away and was silent. Then he turned back. "You got any grub?"

Budrow shook his head. "I'm about done. I gave Ranger the last of the oats tonight. I was going to see if I could find a ranch to ride for until I got some money to move on."

Roads leaned close and looked into Budrow's eyes for a long time. "I reckon you should come with me. My sister and her husband live about forty miles from here. We can get fed and taken care of. Have you ever punched cattle?"

"No, but I'm an excellent rider, and I learn fast."

"Well, some old boys I know, Charlie Goodnight and his pard, Loving, are going to drive some cattle north to the railhead. A fella I rode for before the war, John Southwaite, is hooking up with them. They'll need expert hands. I think you might work out."

"Say, Roads, that's mighty good of you. When do we start?"

"We'll ride to my sister's tomorrow and then over to Charlie's. Better get some shuteye."

"Will Ragland and his boys be back?"

"That owlhoot? He's got no sand. He knows I'd shoot him into ragdolls if he shows his face around me." He leaned close. "Fought for a southern woman's honor, eh?" He spit into the fire. "You know, Budrow, I gotta feeling I might ride the river with you, son."

CHAPTER TWO

RIDERS OF THE RANGE

Garrett Roads could have made his way to the Canadian River and the family ranch near the Llano Estacado blindfolded, in the dead of night, during a blinding rainstorm. His horse, one he had gained in the latter half of the war, could probably find its way to Richmond or any spot in Virginia. But the Texas Panhandle would be a cypher it could not solve. Not yet. In time.

It was dawn. He'd be darned if he hadn't made camp with a dang Yankee. Roads leaned from his saddle and spat. Still, to be honest, the Yankee had made a good cup of coffee from the grounds in his saddlebags. He'd had white sugar to throw into their tin mugs too. A man with white sugar in his pockets in the spring of 1866, after a war that had been too long by half, was a force to be reckoned with.

Impulsively, Roads reached down and patted his gelding's neck. Sharpsburg. What Yankees like Budrow called Antietam. A good solid name for a horse to remind him of a good solid fight, when he'd led a group of good solid men as Lieutenant Roads. That's where he'd earned his nickname. Just like Tom Jackson had earned his at First Manassas. *There are Jackson and his men standing like a stone wall! Rally behind the Virginians!* Roads's sergeant had hollered in much the same way over the roar of musket fire at Sharpsburg. "Lookit, Lieutenant Roads! Steady as a granite boulder no plow can turn! Get behind Roads, boys, and make a fight!"

Budrow interrupted his thoughts as if he'd been reading Roads's mind. "I've told you how I came to be drummed out. How'd you go from officer to corporal?"

Roads looked straight ahead at the miles of April grass lit by morning sun. "I didn't go from officer to corporal. I went from officer to nothing. I was just building myself back up when Lee ended it all at Appomattox. One year ago."

"So maybe you'd have been a captain or major by now?"

Roads crackled a laugh. "Maybe. If you all had put up enough fight. And enough officers above me had swallowed Yankee lead whole."

"But why did they take away your rank to begin with?"

"Huh. That's a story as big as Texas."

"Care to share it?" asked Budrow.

Roads shook his head. "I don't. Some other day a hundred years from now."

"One hundred?"

"Two hundred might be better."

Budrow squinted into the sun. "Riders."

Roads looked to his left. "Six of 'em. Go easy, Budrow. This ain't 1863 no more. I expect it'll be some Texas cowhands wondering what we're up to. Keep your hands clear of your guns."

The silhouettes became bodies. Bulky coats and wide-brimmed hats and long dark bandanas covered half their faces. Despite Roads's advice, Budrow instinctively reached for his cap and ball revolver with his left hand. A shot cracked the air and whipped the slouch hat from his head.

"Next one's in your brain! If you got one!"

It was a woman's voice.

In a moment, the six riders had ringed them.

Two had pistols out.

Roads took note they were Colt Navy Sixes like he wore.

Another rider spoke up, lowering her bandana. Roads took in the freckles, wisps of russet hair, the large eyes, and eyelashes. "You gentlemen will need to drop your gun belts to the ground," she said.

This was not how Roads had expected to be welcomed back to Texas. His back was up. "Supposing I don't, missy."

The redhead's cat-green eyes narrowed sharply. "Don't call me missy, stranger. Killing a man is easy. I've been doing it for the past five years. Both of you, drop your gun belts."

A different woman raised her voice, tugging down her bandana. "We don't waste time looking for tall cottonwoods. We just practice our shooting skills on men like you. Do as Major Paris says."

"Major Paris?" Roads looked around at all six of them. "Are you some sort of military unit?"

"We are the Texas Range Riders," the same woman responded.

Now it was Roads's turn to narrow his gray, gun-steel eyes. "You're not Texas Rangers."

"There are no more Texas Rangers. The Yankee government in Washington, led by that traitor, Andrew Johnson, has brought in Reconstruction. They disbanded the Rangers. But we and other women like us have been guarding this region since our men left to fight for our freedom in '61."

"So, all of you here are women?"

"That's right. And all of us know how to shoot straight. I'm Sergeant Cassidy. Now, for the last time, drop your gun belts."

Roads and Budrow unbuckled their gun belts, reaching down as low as they could before letting them fall.

The woman named Paris moved her buckskin mare closer to Budrow. "Thank you for the Henry rifle, mister. Just ease it out of its scabbard for me."

She'd drawn her pistol. Budrow immediately recognized it as a LeMat, a nine-shot Confederate pistol with a second barrel underneath the regular one. The second barrel fired a charge of 16-gauge buckshot. Paris saw him stare at it for a moment, and the corners of her mouth brought up in a small smile

"I can make a hole in you big enough to drive a locomotive through." She almost laughed. "I've done it before on better men. Give me the Henry."

Budrow gave her the Henry. "As the lady requested."

She took it, holstering her LeMat and pointing the Henry at him. "I'm confident you don't ride with an empty rifle."

"No, ma'am. I do not."

"Neither would I. Now, let's get down to business. What are you gentlemen doing in these parts?"

"Heading home," replied Roads. "Family ranch is just a little ways yonder. By the Canadian."

Paris arched her dark red eyebrows. "Is it?"

"I can supply you with all the names of the members of my family."

"I'm sure you can. Anyone can get the names from a man, kill the man, then pretend to be him with Texicans that don't know any better."

Roads smiled. "Forgive me. We have not made our proper introductions. All those years of warfare have made me lax in my etiquette." He swept off his gray Confederate slouch hat with an exaggerated flourish. "Corporal Garrett Roads, at your service. May I take the opportunity to introduce my traveling companion, Carson Budrow? His friends call him Kit."

Once again, Paris's emerald eyes became slits. "I'm not his friend."

"I told him the very same thing."

"If you're only a corporal, why are you wearing an officer's hat?"

"I was once a lieutenant."

"What happened?"

"That, ma'am, is a story as long as the Pecos."

Paris snorted. So did her horse. "If it's as long as the Pecos, we don't have time for it. Say something smarter."

"I repeat. I am Garrett Roads. My family ranch is Caballos y Hombres. It is situated--"

He did not get any farther. One ranger on a red roan brought her mare nose to nose with his gelding. She tore off her bandana and hat and shook out her silvery hair in a kind of fury. "You're Garrett Roads, you say?"

"I am."

"Do you know who I am?"

"I do not. Other than you are as beautiful as the sunrise."

Her blue eyes flashed like gunfire. "Do not presume to sass me, stranger, or I'll start shooting off your fingers and toes. I've known Garrett Roads since I was twelve years old. I met him in Santa Fe in the company of my father and mother in 1858. In all those eight years, I could never forget him. His face and features are engraved on my mind. You are not him."

"And you are?"

"I am Brandy Black. Captain Brandy Black. Garrett Roads did not have a handlebar moustache. His hair was never so long as yours. Or as unkempt."

"In 1858, I did not have a moustache, no. I was too young. When I left for war in 1861, I did not have a moustache then either, though I was nineteen. But I grew one after Sharpsburg in 1862." He ran a finger along both sides of it. "I do recall the Black family. Your father knew mine well. Robert Smith Black. He is also a cattleman, but closer to the Pecos. Our families dined together. I was sixteen. Ha. I thought I was twenty-one."

Brandy broke into a smile. "Yes, you did." Then doubt swept back in. "You can't be him."

"You were twelve, you say? Skinny as a hoe handle, I recall. Missing two front teeth. Hair like straw tied into three pigtails. Three. I remember thinking that was odd. You had a pink dress with red flowers that fell down as far as your toes."

Brandy's face had grown white.

Roads went on. "You whistled Dixie. Your father said you weren't to whistle. But on the street, after the meal, I saw you by yourself outside the old church, La Parroquia, and at first you were whistling 'Ave Maria.' It was most extraordinary, because your pitch was perfect. And I'd never heard anyone whistle 'Ave Maria' before. Nor have I since. Then you broke into 'Dixie'." Roads laughed. "It's all coming back to me. My, my. Eight years and a war. Look at you. Forgive me, but you truly have grown into a great, shining beauty. And your teeth are perfect."

Captain Brandy Black sat as still as the stars on her roan, silver hair gleaming over her shoulders and chest. "Is there anything else?"

Budrow watched Roads think for a moment. Then saw more light come into his face. The twenty-four-year-old soldier smiled into the blue eyes of the twenty-year-old Texan beauty. His words couldn't have astonished Budrow more, as he sat his horse with his own Henry rifle trained on his heart.

"I gave you a marble," Roads announced. "I must have liked your spirit, because I gave you my best one. It had all the colors of the rainbow."

Brandy nodded. "Yes, it does."

"You don't mean to say you still have it?"

"I do have it, sir." Budrow was quick to pick up on the change in her manner. "I have it right here. I carry it with me. It is my ... it is my good luck charm and my blessing."

She reached into her long riding coat and pulled a small leather pouch into view. They could all see it was hanging from a cord around her neck. She upended the pouch into her palm. Then extended her palm to Roads. He shook his head, hardly believing his eyes, and took it from her gently, his thoughts rushing back to a gangly boy, cocky as a four-star general, trying to catch the eye of the gawky twelve-year-old across the table from him. The marble sparkled in the sun. He turned it over.

"No nicks, no scratches," Roads said. "You must not have played with it."

"Of course not. It is ... it is special to me."

Roads handed it back to her. "I was trying to impress you, you know."

Brandy's thick silver eyebrows arched. "No, you weren't. You were so much older. And I was so ugly."

"Four years seemed like a continent then, I confess. Now it is not even a horse length. Nevertheless. I wanted to impress you. You had the feisty, playful spirit of a foal. I saw that. You weren't ugly, Captain Brandy Black. Different. But never ugly."

Brandy stared at him.

He did not drop his eyes.

It took Major Paris to break the spell. "Gentlemen, it appears we were in error to think you were otherwise than who you are. Two soldiers headed to Caballos y Hombres Ranch after fighting to free us from Northern tyranny. I'm sorry. This was not the welcome you deserved." She handed the Henry rifle back to Budrow. "Please put your gun belts back on and ride with us."

"Where are we riding?" asked Garret.

"We're going to escort you to your ranch on the Canadian and make sure you both arrive there safely. It's the least we can do."

"Why, thank you, Major."

Garrett and Budrow climbed down to retrieve their belts and pistols. Budrow noticed Garrett was reluctant to break off the gaze between himself and Captain Brandy. Budrow looked around for his black slouch hat, picked it up and dusted it off. There was a neat bullet hole clean through the crown. He put the hat back on. A Ranger was smiling down at him. Probably the one who had fired the shot. Budrow nodded and smiled back. He and Garret remounted.

Captain Brandy was still looking at Garret as they walked their horses south. "They called you Granite. I read it in the papers."

"Yes, they did."

"And they still call you that?"

"Some do."

The eight of them rode along quietly, and Budrow brought his horse alongside Garret's. "Thank you for allowing Major Paris to include me in the Confederacy."

Garret grinned. "It's the least I could do, Budrow. You gave me white sugar for my coffee this morning.

CHAPTER THREE

ADOBE WALLS

They rode all day through a chill wind, headed toward the Canadian River. Budrow pulled his coat tighter around his shoulders, never really warming up. Ranger patiently picked his way along the trail, grabbing a mouthful of shortgrass when he could. The women rode well, sitting their saddles like men, their long coats artfully disguising their femininity. A casual observer would have guessed they were a band of cowboys headed south, or perhaps one of the gangs of dark riders that were being seen in the Panhandle's cattle-rich plains as the price for beef slowly rose, turning the Texas Longhorns into gold on the hoof. About mid-afternoon, two of the women split off and headed out to scout their surroundings.

Ahead, Garrett rode next to Captain Black, leaning toward her from time to time to make a comment. Once the Captain's silvery laugh floated back, but mostly the dreary plain was silent, save for the whistle of the wind. The redheaded Major Paris had settled in beside Budrow on the trail, but they kept conversation short. Ahead of them, Budrow could see low hills on the horizon, breaking the monotony of the plains. Grey clouds, the remnants of last night's storm, strung overhead and an occasional drop of rain splatted against his face.

Texas! Spring here is like winter in hell.

Around dusk, the riders came to a bump of a hill in the middle of a lot of flat. At the base of the hill Budrow saw the remains of some crumbling walls. Off to the west, a small creek flowed from the north, running southeasterly. Budrow rode up beside Garrett.

"Somebody used to live here?"

Garrett turned in his saddle. "This is Adobe Walls. Used to be a trading post. Bent, St. Vrain and Company. Back in the forties, they built a log trading post, swapped junk and whiskey for hides. They built an adobe fort here in 1845, but three years later they closed it because the Indians were getting unfriendly and kept stealing their horses. In forty-nine, Old Bent got mad when the Reddies kept killing his cows, so he took dynamite, blew up the fort, and left Texas forever."

Major Paris joined in. "I don't know if you heard, Roads, but there was a big battle here in 1864. A bunch of Comanche and Kiowa were camped here. General Carleton believed they were responsible for attacks on the wagon trains to Santa Fe, so he sent Kit Carson over here to run 'em out. Surprise, surprise. Carson had two hundred and sixty cavalry, seventy-five infantry and a bunch of Utes and Jicarilla Apaches he used for scouts. But he walked right into a much bigger passel of Injuns."

Captain Black spoke up. "Yeah, Carson had to march through a snowstorm. When he got here, he attacked a Kiowa village about four miles over there." She pointed.

Major Paris grinned. "Yep! What Carson didn't know was that there were ten or fifteen villages of Comanches around, and he'd stuck a stick in a hornet's nest. They marched on over here and took up position behind the walls. Pretty soon, about fourteen hundred really mad Injuns were all around him. By the afternoon, that had doubled. They skirmished and did a lot of shooting, but there wasn't many casualties. The next morning Carson packed up and skedaddled back to New Mexico, leaving this part of Texas in the hands of the Comanches."

"What about my sister's ranch? Do they bother her and Joby?"

Major Paris leaned off her horse and spit. "Joby Watkins? That shiftless cow pie? The Injuns laugh at him. He's about as useless as tits on a boar. What did your sister marry that no account for?"

Garrett laughed. "My sister does what she wants, and nobody tells her different. Joby's okay, and I hear he's a pretty good dad ..."

Paris spoke up. "Yeah, but he couldn't ranch his way out of a cotton bag. He and the boy are off hunting most days while your sister runs the ranch. She's a strong lady, and the Kiowa and Comanche respect that. Besides, they're south of the Canadian and stay out of the Comancheria, so the Indians leave them pretty much alone."

They dismounted and Budrow stretched the stiffness out of his back.

Major Paris looked him over. "You ride pretty good, you a pony-soldier in the war?"

Budrow nodded. "Yep, I was in the cavalry."

"Who'd you ride with, Jeb Stuart?"

"Well, I was at Gettysburg, but I didn't ride with Stuart."

"Who then?"

Budrow was about to answer when Roads walked up. "Friend Budrow had a rather checkered history during the war. He was kinda temperamental, so they shipped him around a lot."

Paris looked at Budrow oddly and then turned away to tend her horse. There was a clatter of hoofs and the two scout riders barreled into camp, scattering gravel as they came. One, a hawk-faced woman of about forty, jumped down and came quickly to Major Paris. "We got company, Major." She pointed out into the approaching dusk. "We were out on Bent Creek, and we spotted some riders on the ridge. Kiowa. Probably about ten or fifteen and headed this way."

Paris shouted orders. "Get your horses behind the walls and check your ammo. Get as many guns loaded as you can."

The women leapt off their horses and got them behind the walls. Budrow checked his pistols, making sure they were capped and sealed. Then he pulled out his rifle. Garrett looked it over. "Iron frame, sixteen shot if I'm not mistaken."

Budrow nodded. "Yep, my father gave it to me when I was home after Gettysburg. He knew Winchester and Henry, used to go up to their factory in New Haven. Henry presented this to my father personally."

"Well, I hope you can use it."

"I've been hunting since I was a kid. I know how to shoot." Budrow glanced down at Garrett's holstered guns. "I can handle a pistol, too, but not like you. Maybe if we get out of this scrap, you can show me a thing or two."

Garrett smiled a slow smile. "Why, so you can outdraw me someday?"

Budrow grinned back. "If it ever comes to that, yes."

Major Paris called to them. "I want that Henry at the end of the wall. The rest of us have Spencers with only seven shots. So, I want your fire going across them when we have to reload. Roads, take a rifle and get down at the other end and make sure they don't flank us."

Budrow moved down the wall and stood by Major Paris. He watched Ranger. In a minute Ranger's ears went up and flicked to the left into the gathering darkness.

Budrow pointed his Henry that way. "They're coming in over there and they are after the horses."

Paris looked at Budrow. "How do you know …?"

Just then, there was a soft sound, and an arrow came whistling out of the dark. It took Major Paris high in the shoulder, and she went down with a surprised moan.

"Garrett! Over here!" Garrett came on the run. The two men saw dark shapes moving toward them. The two rifles barked as one and there was a shriek, followed by a grunting sound. Another shape shifted in the dark, and Budrow took the brave down with a shot to the head. More arrows came out of the dark. By now, the women were firing. There were howls as the hail of bullets hit home. The Kiowa, surprised by the firepower of their intended victims, fired some more arrows and then slipped away. Garrett nodded to the hawk-faced woman and the two of them slipped over the wall and disappeared into the dark. Budrow looked down at Major Paris and quickly knelt beside her. She was lying on her side, but she didn't make a sound. The arrow had gone partway through and protruded out her back. She looked up at Budrow. There were tears in her eyes, but her face was set like flint.

"I've got to open your coat and shirt, break it off and pull it through."

Paris nodded. "Do it."

Budrow opened her coat and then hesitated at the shirt buttons. Paris reached with her good hand and tore the shirt open. The pale skin of her breast gleamed in the fading light. The arrow had gone in just above. A stream of blood marred the smooth white skin.

"Ain't you ever seen one of those, Budrow?" She smiled.

Budrow took hold of the arrow. "Ready?" She nodded again.

He snapped the feathered end off with one quick move.

She gasped but did not scream.

"Take a deep breath, Major. I'm going to pull it through now."

She blinked the tears back and took a deep breath. Budrow pulled with a quick motion and the arrow came out. Paris gasped and fainted.

Garrett came back out of the darkness. "They're gone. Dragged their dead and wounded with them. Looks like we killed some. There was a lot of blood. They won't be back. How's the Major doing?"

"She's got sand, that's for certain. Didn't make a sound when I pulled that arrow out."

Captain Black came over and knelt. "Nettie? Nettie?"

Nettie Paris opened her eyes. "Howdy, Brandy."

"Howdy yourself, Nettie."

Brandy looked at the wound. "Better cauterize that so it won't get infected."

Paris groped in her pocket and pulled out a brass loader, gave it to Brandy, who poured some powder in the wound. "Got a match, Budrow?"

Budrow looked at her. Her eyes blazed. "Light it, Budrow."

Budrow reached in his pocket and pulled out a match. He struck it on his thumbnail and put it on the powder. There was a flash, and Nettie groaned and went limp.

Budrow looked at her face. "She passed out again, but she'll be all right. I need something to bind this with."

Captain Black handed over a piece of cloth. Budrow tore it into strips and quickly bound the Major's shoulder. Then he pulled her shirt together and fastened it.

Nettie groaned again and opened her eyes. Her face was pale, and Budrow noticed for the first time that with her hat off and her face exposed, she was very beautiful. Her red hair framed a symmetrical face, and her eyes were a brilliant green. Budrow reached down with a leftover piece of cloth and wiped her lips. He inspected the cloth. "No blood, Nettie. The arrow missed your lung. Looks like you'll just have a sore shoulder for a few weeks. And a nice little round scar to mark the occasion."

She smiled weakly and tried to get up, but Brandy pushed her back down. "We'll camp here tonight, Major. I'll get your bedroll." She nodded at Garrett. "Let's get a fire going."

Garrett turned and went to look for some greasewood. Brandy went to Nettie's horse and returned with a bedroll. Budrow started to stand up, but Nettie took his hand. "Put your roll next to mine ... Kit."

Budrow smiled.

In the morning, they shared some dried beef and a little coffee, then saddled the horses. Nettie was still weak, so Budrow lifted her up on Ranger and climbed into the saddle behind her. He marked she was light as a feather, a slip of a thing under her heavy coat. Nettie leaned back into his arms.

"We're twenty miles from the ranch, you don't mind?"

"My pleasure, ma'am."

The riders headed south and as they rode, Budrow thought on Nettie's words of the night before.

Yeah, I've seen one of those before.

A picture came unbidden, the lovely Annette Devereaux, standing stripped to the waist with the pitchfork in her hands, desperately trying to fend off the three Union soldiers in the barn outside Atlanta. Budrow had walked in on the scene when he came to care for Ranger.

"What are you men doing?"

The leader, a swarthy private named Jansen, had turned to him with an evil grin. "We just havin' a little fun, Captain. None of us has had a woman for a long time, and she's a real beauty."

Budrow's gun had come out. "You men stop what you're doing and get back to camp."

Jansen smiled again. "The hell we will, Captain. Why don't you get in line and you can have the leftovers." He turned and nodded to his friends, and then they all lunged toward Budrow. There was a flash and a roar, and Jansen's grin was joined by a round red hole between his eyes. The other two were still coming. Budrow's Colt roared again, and the second man went down. The third soldier turned and ran out the door. Budrow turned toward the woman who was trying to cover her nakedness. He remembered the trembling lips, the beautiful violet depths of her eyes, the gratitude written on her face like a book.

"You're pretty quiet, Budrow," Nettie whispered. "Somethin' on your mind?"

Budrow hesitated and then took a deep breath. "No, nothing."

CHAPTER FOUR

SKIN RICKETTS

Garrett would tell everybody who would listen that getting back to Texas was as hard as fighting Grant, Sherman, and Sheridan together on a bad day with a crippled mount, an empty pistol, and a broken saber.

First, there had been Budrow's near-lynching. Then the well-armed and feisty women called the Texas Range Riders had put the drop on him and Budrow and almost filled them with lead. After that had been the Kiowa attack and almost losing the handsome Major Nettie Paris to a well-aimed arrow—a grief for all but especially the smitten Yankee that Garrett had dragged into North Texas with him. Garrett himself had just gotten to the point in his thoughts where he realized the mesmerizing Captain Brandy Black and he might have future possibilities, hang any commitments he might have made prior to the War of Northern Aggression, when a string of cowboys seemed to emerge out of the folds of land and come at them hell-bent for leather.

"What's this?" demanded Budrow, immediately tugging out his Henry.

"Danged if I know," muttered Garrett as he pulled his Navy Sixes. "But it reminds me of a Yankee cavalry charge."

"Them ain't no low life blue bellies," snarled Paris. "That's Skin Ricketts and his gang, and he's been trying this crap since First Manassas. I don't know what it is about this trip to the Canadian, but after those Kiowa and now Ricketts, I'm expecting a twister out of season."

"He always do it this way?" asked Garrett. "No cover and right at ya?"

"Look around you, corporal. There isn't any cover. He just jumps and kills, which is why they call him Jumping Ricketts."

"Why'd you say he was Skin?"

"That's the name he got for skinning his enemies alive. Even the Comanche avoid this rattlesnake."

"I don't think we'll have the opportunity to avoid," hissed Budrow as he levered a cartridge into the chamber of his Henry rifle. "Is Texas always this wild, Major Paris?"

She shot a grin at him just before he squeezed the trigger. "Mister, you ain't seen nothin' yet."

Budrow fired and fired and fired again. The Rangers scattered, shooting at the desperadoes with their pistols and rifles. Garrett counted twelve owlhoots and wondered what they wanted badly enough to charge into a wall of bullets. As if he had said it out loud, Brandy Black spat: "They want our horses and weapons and ammo. That's what matters to them."

"What will they do with us?"

"What do you think? They've got no use for prisoners."

"There's only twelve of them. The eight of us can take 'em."

"Ricketts has got more than this crew. I just don't know where."

She galloped away from Garrett as one of the Rangers was shot from her horse. He gave the woman a brief glance and saw she was stone dead. The bullet had opened her skull. It might as well have been a skirmish during the war with all the shouting and shooting. "Dang," he muttered, sinking into his saddle so that he was a harder target. "I was supposed to come home to peace."

The Rangers quickly blasted four or five of the gang out of Texas and beyond the moon. They were deadly shots and not afraid to trade blows with the outlaws, bullet for bullet and face to face. Or fist to fist. It surprised him to see Black launch herself from her horse at an outlaw twice her size, knock him out of the saddle, pin him when they hit the ground and begin pummeling him with hard, fast punches that left him stunned. Then Garrett saw the silver flash of a Bowie and the man's final cry of pain.

A moment later, Garrett spotted Sergeant Cassidy, who couldn't have been over five foot nothing, leap in the saddle behind one of the outlaws as he barreled towards Paris, pistol sparking. She wrapped her arm around his neck, squeezed with all her might, which Garrett quickly saw was not inconsiderable, made the owlhoot drop his pistol, and reached around with her free hand to seize the reins. She wrenched the man's head sharply to the left and kicked his body out of the saddle, his neck limp and dangling, driving the horse straight at another gang member, sending his mount crashing to the earth with him underneath. He screamed as the weight of the horse broke his bones and ribs, and she was kind enough to shoot him in the head.

"Well, hell," growled Garrett, watching the mayhem as the Range Riders shot Ricketts's gang to pieces or beat them to death, "these Texas ladies sure don't need my help or the Yankee's. They are as tough and rough as John Bell Hood's Texas Brigade at Sharpsburg."

But he saw a second Ranger shot out of the saddle right beside Brandy Black and twisted around quickly to spot the shooter, both pistols ready. Ten more outlaws were coming at them from behind, all of them firing Henry rifles. A bullet took off his hat, and another whipped one of his Colts out of his hand, making his arm sting. A third Ranger flew backwards off her horse and Garrett grit his teeth. They were in it for it now, and only a few rifles between them. He made a mental note to procure a Henry at his earliest opportunity. If he survived this gun battle. Which had been going well, and in their favor, and now wasn't.

He heard a blood-chilling scream and twisted in his saddle again, trying to locate the source. The source pelted right past him at full steam, still shrieking from the back of his horse and firing his Henry at the fresh attackers as swiftly as he could lever it. Budrow. Just like a cavalry charge. Well, God in heaven, if a lowdown Yankee could give a rebel yell and go pell-mell at the enemy without regard for life or limb, then Garrett Roads would not be denied. He might only have a pistol with four shots left, but he still had his saber strapped to a saddlebag and he reached down to tug it loose as he spurred his horse forward. He caught up to Budrow and shouted, "You never got your fill of cavalry charges in the war, Billy Yank?"

"I never charged with the likes of you, Johnny Reb!"

"So how is this going to work?"

"We're going to tear them to pieces, Granite!"

"The same thought crossed my mind, Kit! Yeeeeaaaaarrrrryaaaaaaayooooooo!" Garrett swung his saber and hollered at the top of lungs. "Let's get 'em, boys!"

"Let's git 'em!" yelled Budrow.

A bullet opened up Garrett's cheek, another took a chunk off his ear, a third ripped across his forehead. The blood that ran into his eyes almost blinded him, but that did not prevent the cavalryman from emptying three saddles with four shots point blank and emptying two more with fierce slashes of his saber. Off his right shoulder, as if he were in some sort of competition with Garrett, Budrow cut off the head of one man with his long Union saber, opened the stomach of a second and removed the arm and leg of a third, while firing his revolver with the other hand, taking out two outlaws with two shots. Blood soaked his left sleeve and left leg and there were angry powder burns all over his face. The women roared up at full gallop, but there was nothing for them to do but look at the bodies that littered the dust.

Paris grunted. "That's a tidy five minutes' work. Were you boys back at Chancellorsville in your heads?"

Both Budrow and Granite were panting so hard from battle exertion they couldn't speak.

"Too much blood," Paris suddenly said. "Get them down and get it stopped."

Several of the women easily lifted Budrow and Garrett to the ground and swiftly used bandannas to staunch the flow.

Garrett looked up at Paris. "What about your Rangers, Major?"

Her face was stone. "We lost two. Sergeant Cassidy is wounded in the arm but she's still strong and in the saddle."

"I'm sorry."

She nodded. "Thank you, mister."

"The outlaws?"

"We took care of them our way. Just like you took care of them your way. It was a pleasure."

"Skin Ricketts?"

She spat in the dust. "Jumping Ricketts? He lit out with his right-hand man, Cobb. But his day will come. I swear to heaven it will. I look forward to it."

"Why do I get the feeling this was more than a raid to pick up horses and ammo?"

"They've been wanting to rub us out since we formed the unit. We've sent a number of his men to Satan's hell since the war started. I'm glad we sent a bunch more today."

"So, there's revenge in the cards."

"There's always been revenge in the cards."

Brandy Black was helping with Budrow and Garrett but lingering over Garrett. "All the lead went clean through both of 'em. Two lucky troopers."

Paris cocked a thick eyebrow. "Two tough troopers. And darned heroic. That charge stirred my blood."

Black smiled down at Garrett. "Mine too."

"Can they ride?"

"They've lost blood and I'm not sure ..."

"I can ride!" Both men said it at the same time.

Paris fought smiling but couldn't help herself. "If I didn't know better, I'd think you two staged that charge to impress the ladies. Well, sirs, we're not easily impressed, certainly not by men. But I have to say, riding into a storm of bullets, waving those swords and dishing out the rebel yell? That did the trick." She reined her horse aside so that they couldn't see the shine in her eyes. "Mount up, boys. We got a good ways to go yet, and we can't have you slowing us down. And make sure you get a lot of water into you." After a few minutes, she put her horse alongside Garrett's. "Your friend has sand."

Garrett smoothed down his moustache with two fingers, wincing when the horse stumbled. "I can't call him a friend. Just met him a few days back. We threw in together."

"What do you know about him?"

"Not much."

"How much is not much? He doesn't have a Southern accent."

"I know he was an officer. I know they stripped him of his rank for shooting two of his men during the war."

"What! Why?"

"Because, Major Paris, they were raping a woman. He defended her. The army saw it otherwise."

Paris was silent, taking this information in. "And he agreed to move cattle with you?"

"He did."

"Just like that?"

"Well, ma'am, he was hereabouts anyways."

Paris examined Garrett with jade green eyes. "What aren't you telling me?"

"You want me to write y'all a book?"

"Maybe you can just tell me one thing today and then tomorrow a second thing, Granite."

"I'll do my best. But shouldn't you be talking to Budrow?"

"Not about this."

"All right. Shoot."

Paris looked straight ahead, and her face was cut rock. "So, do you know if ... if ..."

She didn't want to say it.

Garrett didn't help her out.

It was her problem, and he was weak and in too much pain from the holes the outlaws had put in him.

Suddenly, she expelled a gust of air and blurted, "Does he have someone, Granite?"

Garrett sat on this a bit. Then he replied, "That I don't know. We really haven't talked about lovers. Like I said, Budrow fell in with me, but he ain't no friend of mine."

"Has he ... has he ..."

Garrett waited, but there wasn't anything more. He saw a patch of blood on her shirt from the arrow wound and softened up. He expected she was in as much pain as he was, or maybe more. "Yeah, he has. Not in so many words. But that man has cottoned to you, Major. I'd say it's pretty bad. I thought a few bullet holes might cure him. But." He grinned at her. "I reckon he's worse now than he ever was."

She snapped her face towards him. "Why do you say that?"

"Why do you think he rode straight at those desperadoes, knowing it was certain death?"

"I …"

"It wasn't for me. And while I know he cares about your whole crew, he didn't do it for them either."

"Granite…"

"He'd have killed them all on his own, Major. He was so full of spit and fire, he didn't need me. He did it to protect you."

"I don't need a man to protect me."

"Well, ma'am, you got one. You were wounded and hurting, and he wasn't going to let them get anywhere near you. It was the same as the woman he saved. He didn't give a hoot if they court-martialed him. He did the right thing, even though it cost him. Same thing here. It might have cost him everything. But it was the right thing. Maybe not mine or yours. But it was his. So, he charged and threw his life to the Texas wind."

"But you joined him."

"I sure did. He may not be a friend, but I know a brave man when I see one, and I had no intention of letting him die alone."

"How can he like me that much so fast?"

Garrett smiled at her. "Looked in your big oval mirror lately, ma'am? Listened to your own voice? Watched the way you move? The way you sit a saddle? You're savvy, tough, beautiful, and strong. You're the best of Texas in one woman. No one on God's green earth would have a difficult time believing a man with a heart like Budrow's would fall fast and hard for a woman with a heart like yours. No one."

Nettie Paris rode quietly for several minutes, making a point of not looking at him or over to her left at Budrow.

Then she asked Garrett, "Can we bury our women at your ranch?"

Garrett touched his hat brim. "Captain Paris, it would be an honor."

CHAPTER FIVE

CROSSING THE CANADIAN

Carson Budrow was troubled. He had a battle going on in his head—a battle worse than Gettysburg. For months, the face and body of Annette Devereaux had haunted his dreams. He remembered her, stripped to the waist, a pitchfork in her hands, backed against the wall of the barn, holding off the three Yankee troopers intent on raping her. Her eyes were blazing, and her dark hair spilled over her shoulders, leaving little to his imagination. But it was her eyes that had captured him—the French fire of her Cajun birth burning in the violet depths. He knew if he had not come, she would have killed herself rather than being dishonored by Yankee scum. And the gratitude in her eyes as he covered her nakedness and they stepped around the dead bodies of the two men he had gunned down for her sake.

But now, as he rode, another face imposed itself over the face of Annette Devereaux—the fair face of Nettie Paris. She had laughed at him when he had to expose her breast to pull the arrow out, but there had been a blush on her face, the blush of a modest woman who has kept her honor and nobility in the heat of life on the Texas plains. And she had captured him too. And so now the battle raged.

"Blast it!"

Garrett Roads looked over and grinned. "Those gunshot wounds getting to you, Budrow, or is it something else?"

"Hey, for a Reb who says he ain't my friend, you're getting mighty personal, Stonewall."

Roads laughed. "Okay, okay. Don't take offense. I just noticed you was mooning after the red-headed major. Just between you and me, I think you should cozy up to that gal. You won't find better in Texas."

"Well, Texas is only one state, Roads."

"Ah, thinking about the beautiful daughter of the south that you saved from dishonor?"

Budrow spit some dust out of his mouth. "I never said she was beautiful."

Road grinned again. "Didn't have to, Budrow. Saw the look on yer face."

Budrow looked over and spit again. "You know, that grin is getting on my nerves." He spurred Ranger into a trot and left Roads to eat his dust.

Around noon, they approached a crossing where the river came out of a deep canyon. The canyon wall stretched north and west. In front of them it turned south and continued, its face irregular and incised by washes and ravines.

"That there is the eastern wall of the Llano Estacado, what the Spaniards called the Staked Plains. They called it that because that wall runs all the way into New Mexico, like a fence. About two thousand feet up on top is the driest, most miserable, God-forsaken country you every laid eyes on. Even the Injuns don't cross it much, except at two or three places." He pointed south. "The wall heads thataway, and from here it's called the Caprock Escarpment. You get up there and all you got is a big nothin'. No rocks, no trees, no shrubs, no animals, and worst of all, not a drop of water."

Budrow shook his head. "Why would anyone go up there?"

Roads grinned. "If you had no other choice. My Uncle Jim got chased up there by a bunch of Mescalero Apaches, up from Mexico on a raid for horses. My dad and Jim were out hunting, and they got separated by the Apaches. Jim took off west. My dad went east. They had Jim trapped, so he skedaddled up one of these canyons and got up on top. The Apaches followed him up because they wanted his horse and the packhorse running with him that had a fresh killed deer on it. My dad watched him go up, and he just knew he'd never see Jim again. Well, Uncle Jim headed south along the rim with the Apaches hot on him. He cut that packhorse loose, and the Indians went after it. Jim had a great horse, a wiry little mustang that could go four days without water and bring a dead man out of the desert. With the Indians following the deer meat, he got a jump on them." Garrett stopped to pull out the makings for a smoke.

Budrow was interested now. "Well, what happened, for gosh sakes?"

Garrett finished rolling his smoke, struck a match, and then looked over at Budrow.

"Uncle Jim rode that little horse into the ground. Then he set out walking with the Apaches still on his trail. He comes to a big ravine across the trail. Couldn't go back, couldn't go forward. Injuns coming on him." He took a long drag.

"Roads, tell me what happened!"

Garrett shrugged. "They killed him and scalped him."

Budrow scowled. "What? Killed him?"

The ladies around the two riders burst into laughter at the look of dismay on Budrow's face. Captain Black rode by and tipped her hat. "You shore got that greenhorn, Garrett. Uncle Jim! Ha ha! Hey, Carson, Roads never had an Uncle Jim. But he's been tellin' that story for years to any fool that would listen."

Budrow looked at Roads. "That makes us even, Granite."

Around sundown, they rode into a small valley. The sun was disappearing over the rim but was still lighting the sky with glorious bands of orange, pink, and blue. A trail ran down through a stand of trees, and beyond that, on a little rise, a large spread-out ranch house stood. Smoke was coming from the chimney. There was a big barn, plenty of outbuildings, and the pastures close to the house were fenced. Budrow looked around. A small stream ran by the house and wended its way into the canyon. Tall grass lined the stream, and fat cattle fed contentedly. It was warmer down in the valley. Budrow could hear doves talking in the trees, and a flock of swallows flew by looking for bugs. Just as the sun went down over the rim, a shaft of light came through a cut in the wall and lit the area around the house with a shimmering glow.

Nettie rode up beside Budrow. "This here's the Watkins ranch. Prettiest spread in the whole panhandle. Used to be called the Roads Place. Garrett's dad found this valley back in 1845. When he died, he knew Garrett was a wanderer, so he left it to Alice. Then that Joby Watkins came along and sweet-talked her into marryin' him. Now he sits around on his rear end drinking or goes hunting while she runs the place. I tell you, Budrow, Texas would be nothing without strong women."

Budrow thought back to his own cultured upbringing in Philadelphia. Women with pale faces and low-cut gowns, men with brandy and cigars talking about the future of the west and the money to be made. "I'm beginning to see what you mean."

Major Paris looked him up and down. "You got one, Budrow?"

"One what?"

"A good woman?"

Budrow felt himself blushing, but he looked straight into the deep green eyes and smiled. "That's an awkward kind of question, Major."

"Why's that, Budrow? Do I scare you? Out here, women aren't afraid to ask awkward questions."

Just then, a woman came out on the porch, drying her hands on her apron. Tall, a strong face, dark hair cut short behind her ears. The dying sun lit a halo around her face. She put her hand up to shade her eyes and spotted the women riders.

"Hey, ladies! Brandy! Nettie! You're just in time for dinner. We got plenty of stew."

Captain Black swung off her horse. "And we got some fixin's to add to it, Alice, but we got to get the horses settled."

"Turn 'em loose in the pasture, Brandy. There's plenty of grass. And dust wallows to roll in."

"We also got two of our compadres who are now riding the sunset trail. Can we lay 'em out in the barn and bury 'em tomorrow?"

Alice nodded. "Pleased to have you put them out in the graveyard with my mom and pop."

"And Uncle Jim?" Roads said as he swung off his horse.

Alice took a long look at Roads as the rest of the rangers laughed. "Well, well, Ulysses, the wanderer returns to Ithaca. Did it take these ladies to get you safely across Texas?"

"Mighty stingy words, sister, especially when your long-lost prodigal brother has returned to the old homestead looking for a kiss and some stew."

"You old catfish," Alice grinned, and came off the porch and leaped up into Garrett's arms. She delivered the requested kiss and held him long in her arms. Finally, she pulled away.

"Garrett, Garrett, I missed you. What in blue blazes took you so long? And who's your handsome friend?"

Garrett turned to Budrow. "Climb down from there, Budrow, and meet Alice, the best rider, best shot, and meanest cow puncher this side of the Pecos. Alice, this here is Budrow, Carson Budrow. He says his friends call him Kit, but none of us are calling him that yet."

Brandy and Nettie snickered, but Alice stepped up to Budrow. She looked him over and then looked into his eyes. After they stood that way for a minute, she held out her hand. "Nice to meet you, Kit. I think I'd like to be your friend."

Budrow felt his shoulders relax.

This is a woman I could get to like.

Just then, a man came out on the porch. He was in an undershirt and had two days' growth of beard on his face. A boy about twelve, it seemed, peeked around the doorframe.

"Well, I'll be hornswaggled! If it ain't the prodigal returned. Come to get the ranch back, Garrett?"

Alice turned in a flash. "Shut up, Joby. You're drunk. If you're going to be unsociable, you can spend the night in the barn.

Joby started to say something, but Alice put her hand on the pistol Budrow had just noticed she was carrying on her hip. "You got something to say, Joby?"

The man waved his hands and grinned. "No, Alice, now be nice. I was just playing around. Good to see you, Garrett. Come on in. You know where your old room is."

Garrett walked up on the porch. "Howdy, Jimmy, you gonna come say hello?"

The boy stepped out onto the porch and up to Garrett. "Howdy, Uncle Garrett, shore is good to see you. Been a long time."

They shook hands, and then, the boy leaped up into his uncle's arms. Garrett laughed and swung the boy around. "Man, youngster, you have growed. You're most a man." He set the boy down.

"You gonna tell us about the war? Did you kill any Yankees? My dad says any Yankee that ever lived should die with worms and rot in hell."

Garrett looked down at the boy. "The war's over, Jimmy."

"Not out here, it ain't," snarled Joby.

Garrett shot a cutting look at Alice's husband. "What in the Sam hell do you know about it, Joby? I didn't see you fighting for Texas." Joby muttered and went back inside. Garrett looked down at Jimmy. "Like I said, the war's over. And what we got to do is quit the hating and put the country back together. I'm sure you'd find that there are a few Yankees who might not have to rot in hell."

His eyes found Budrow's over the boy's shoulder.

CHAPTER SIX

THE SOUTHWAITES

Garrett Roads was on his horse, sipping from a tin cup of coffee, when Carson Budrow walked out of the ranch house door.

"It's so early," Budrow complained, "and so dark, even the birds aren't singing yet."

"Mm." Roads had another swallow. "They're just like people. They'll sing when they have something to sing about."

"Like a sunrise."

"Sure. A sunrise. But a morning is more than a sunrise." Roads pointed with his chin. "I had one of the hands saddle up your mare, Ranger. Alice has a few boys that use the old bunkhouse. Joby ain't nothing but an empty sack. She needs their help to keep things running."

Budrow swung up onto his horse. "When did the Range Riders leave?"

"They haven't left. Just moved on into the barn last night while you were snoring. Found the ranch house too cozy, I guess."

"Where are we headed?"

"There's some people I want you to meet. Ranch isn't far. Little over an hour's ride."

"Do you think the ladies will still be here once we get back?" asked Budrow.

Roads grinned. "Head and heart are both spinning? Well, God is smiling down on your Yankee soul because Major Paris and her crew intend to hang around Roads Place for a couple of days. Said they wanted to scout around."

"I thought it was the Watkins Ranch?"

"It'll never be that to me. The sooner Joby is out of this family, the better."

"How do you intend to arrange that?"

"I'm no assassin. But maybe the Comanche will help me out. Or a handsome stranger from one of those dime westerns people have started reading. *The Blazing Guns of Kid Pecos*."

They both laughed as they walked their horses out onto a dirt track that was half trail and half grass. The graveyard was just to their right. The fresh mounds of earth were obvious.

"I'm sorry to see that," said Budrow.

Roads nodded. "There will be payday for Skin Ricketts. But I thank you for making sure that job was done."

Budrow feigned surprise. "I didn't do anything."

Roads smiled. "I'll admit I was a bit pained when I heard you'd gone ahead without me. I was jawing with Alice. Didn't even hear the clink of a spade. But Major Paris said she'd asked you for your help. My thinking is I have a Yankee here who is three times over a full moon for that Texican gal. You'd do anything she asked. She said you dug so fast it was as if you were expecting an artillery barrage. She is mighty grateful."

"It was my pleasure to lend them a hand. No. My honor."

"The day will come when she shows her gratitude, Budrow. My advice? Take it. However it comes, do not push her away. That would be an insult no Texas woman would bear with grace. Accept it. And thank the good Lord in heaven for the gift of a woman's fancy."

"They dug too," Budrow argued.

Roads shook his head. He was just finishing his coffee. "No matter. The major said you did the lion's share."

Budrow smiled, and then, the smile stopped. "There wouldn't be any gratitude if she knew I was a no-good Yankee."

"True. She might throw down for a knife fight with y'all instead. This is a problem I have not yet solved in my head. I have asked God for help. No, I mean it, I truly have. I expect we could use some kind of divine intervention. Like you Yanks benefited from on the afternoon of July 3, 1863."

Budrow snorted. "There was no divine intervention. Pickett sent his men into a firestorm. Did he think his soldiers weren't flesh and blood?"

"That assault was the bad side of Southern chivalry. Pickett blames Lee for ordering the attack to this day. We have glamorized it. That is our way. We think heroism and gallantry are impervious to shellfire. I recall you all thought the same at Fredericksburg. July 3rd will go down in history as something brave and majestic. Like the Alamo. That is how we cover up war's wounds and bloody losses. We immortalize them."

Budrow looked over at Roads. "You are waxing eloquent today."

"Yes, indeed. I would like to rewrite all bad and bloody history and make it something better. In fact, I wouldn't mind running Texas one day. I think I could do some good."

Budrow stared. "As a politician?"

Roads laughed sharply. "Not at all. As a statesman in the finest clothes." His tin coffee cup had a leather strap on its handle. He looped it over his saddle horn. "I must confide something. Where we are headed, there is a headstrong woman. I must add she is a glamourous, resplendent, headstrong woman who stopped my heart frequently before I left for the war. Oh, and she knew it too. Knew what she could do to me. Knew she had me between her thumb and forefinger and could play with me to her heart's delight ... stretch me, squeeze me, roll me up ... and laugh quite gaily while she went about breaking my heart over and over again."

"And you permitted her to do that to you, Garrett Roads?"

"Permitted? You talk as if I had any sort of control over the situation. I not only permitted her to toy with my passions, Budrow, I welcomed it. As much as it hurt, I was so bewitched by her charms it did not matter to me how she tortured my heart, so long as I could be in her company. It was my intention to return a war hero and ask for her hand. It is still my intention."

"You think she will throw herself at your feet because you are Granite Roads now?"

"She will never throw herself at any man's feet. But I hope I may have gained some of her respect. That she will take me seriously and see me as a man and not the boy who was besotted with her loveliness five years ago."

"What is her name?" Budrow asked.

"Ann," Roads replied. "Ann Southwaite. Her father is John Southwaite. Tall as Stone Mountain in Georgia. I saw the mountain once, and he certainly resembles it. That is the man I am taking you to meet. But Ann will be there, most assuredly."

"Is his ranch large?"

"His ranch is bigger than mine, than Roads Place, though I do not know how he has fared after four years of warfare. My sister last saw him six months ago and thought he had lost some of the snap to his long-legged stride. However, I think the message I sent his way will put some red blood back in his veins. He knows Charles Goodnight, and he will want to be part of a cattle drive that puts real money in his pocket once again. John is a good man to have around when the wind blows hard from the north."

Budrow cleared his throat. "I need to tell you something."

Roads stared at him. "You need to tell me something? Then out with it, Budrow."

"The women want to ride with us."

"The women want to ride with us? Which women? Ride where?"

"During the burial last evening. Major Paris and Sergeant Cassidy expressed their desire to push that herd north with us."

"What? No. No. Out of the question, Budrow. This is rough and tumble. Like war, it is man's work."

"I doubt they will take no for an answer, Roads. I expect they can handle anything a man can handle and more. I didn't know what to say in reply."

Roads was adamant. "I told you. It's no. No. What were you thinking?"

Budrow half-laughed. "You make it sound as if they were asking for permission, Roads. They weren't. They were telling me. Your friend--"

"My friend?"

"What else should I call her? Captain Black."

"Brandy!"

"Yes, Brandy, beautiful, silver-haired Brandy. She said they'd follow us the entire way and pick up strays and eat dust if they had to, but they would drive the herd with us, and we had no say in the matter. They'd do as they pleased. And that she'd whip any man in a fight who tried to stop them."

Roads was both surprised and pleased. "She said that?"

Budrow nodded. "We had finished the burial, said our prayers, and were on our way back to the ranch house when all this came up. Her eyes sparked like flint and steel that God Almighty had struck. I think she'd have thrown a punch and knocked me flat if I'd started arguing with her. Anyway, Roads, why would I argue against the possibility of seeing Major Paris every day for two or three months? That's like heaven on earth."

Roads was not swayed. "I can't see it, Budrow, these are Texas ladies--"

"Who has been guarding the borders of your state since 1861? You saw how they put the drop on us. You saw how they roughed up Skin Rickett's gang. You don't think they can herd cattle through thick and thin and much more?"

"Goodnight won't agree with it."

"As if they'd care what he says or thinks. Brandy says to me, 'You're just a passel of men. You don't get to decide what we do or don't do. We can have a pleasant ride together or you all can get dusted down and hurt. Which is it you want?' But that's not your biggest problem, Roads."

Roads stared. "Seems pretty big to me, Billy Yank? What's bigger?"

Budrow thought he would not smile but did. "Choosing between her and Ann Southwaite."

Roads reined up. "I don't have to choose."

Budrow kept going. "Yes, you do. If I'm smitten with Major Paris--"

"Smitten? You're not just smitten, man. You're all of you on fire."

"I'm not denying it. But you? You're doubly smitten with Captain Brandy Black."

"I'm not, Budrow."

"You are, sir, you are. Is that their ranch ahead? You will know the moment you lay eyes on Ann. I don't care if she outshines your Texas sun. The moment you lay eyes on her, you will compare her to Captain Black, and Ann Southwaite will lose. For this thing I know is true from what I've seen and what you've told me. Brandy Black wants you. Ann Southwaite doesn't."

Roads wanted to argue, wanted to yell. But they were close enough he could see John Southwaite and his wife standing on their porch along with their four daughters and two sons. He kept his mouth shut, steamed as he was at the no-good, big-mouthed dang Yankee riding with him. They reined up and Ann, the tallest of the girls, shone out like handfuls of silver and gold. She smiled at Roads the way she'd always smiled at him. Like she knew she had him tightly wrapped around her little finger and snug in the pocket of her dress for all time. Roads smiled back and swept off his Confederate slouch hat: "Miss Southwaite. I am home." But what he really wanted to do was punch Budrow squarely on the jaw and knock him from his saddle, and if he got up, Roads wanted to jump down from his horse and hit him again. Just for being right, and annoyingly so. Roads *was* thinking of Brandy Black. And she was the equal of Ann Southwaite in every respect. Perhaps more than equal. God take that Yankee's soul and burn it.

The ten of them had a brief lunch together at the massive table in the dining hall. Ann drew Roads in with her eyes whenever she had the chance, and he was well aware she wanted him to know he was still hers to do with as she pleased. There was no escaping her powers. It was a fifteen-minute ride to Charlie Goodnight's spread with John Southwaite and Budrow and the whole time, Roads barely heard a word John said about the cattle drive. He was thinking of Brandy, he was thinking of Ann, back and forth. Even when he shook hands with Goodnight, his mind was with the two women who had bested him more than Grant's entire Yankee army had ever done. Only when Goodnight offered him a cigar did he find himself planted by the fireplace in the main room of the ranch house. The man, who looked as if he were fashioned from iron rails, was rumbling, "I intend to start as soon as is practicable. We only need to round up the cattle that will make the drive. Are you boys with me?" He looked hard and straight into Roads's eyes. "Are you with me, son?"

Roads gathered himself in from all the places his mind had been. "I am. As God is my witness, I am with you all the way to Kansas. I will not flinch from my duty, sir."

CHAPTER SEVEN

PILGRIMS

Annette Devereaux brushed a huge horsefly off her arm. It had just started to bite and there was a trace of blood on her smooth skin where she had swept it away. She wiped the blood off and shifted on the uncomfortable wooden seat. The scorching sun burned down on the wagon seat and beads of sweat rolled down her skin. The team of mules walked slowly behind the wagon in front of them.

If Mama could only see her princess sweating! How unladylike.

Annette chuckled to herself, and her father, sitting on the pitching seat beside her, looked over. "What's funny, princess?"

Annette just shook her head. "I was just thinking if Mama could see me now, she would be horrified. I am actually perspiring."

Her father smiled too. "Ah yes, your mama. She was so circumspect in her ways. Women didn't sweat, men didn't belch, at least in the presence of ladies, and Southern belles stayed out of the sun so as not to lose their lily-white skin."

Annette looked down at her arm. She had given up dresses when they crossed the Missouri just after they started out, and she almost drowned when her long dress got tangled in the wheels of the wagon. Now she wore men's pants and woolen shirts, another thing that would have horrified her mother. The skin of her arm was no longer lily white but browned by the sun where it was not covered by her shirt. Her face was also brown even though she had attempted to cover it with a veil when starting her chores. But the veil just captured dust and made everything more uncomfortable, so she gave it up and surrendered to the reality of becoming a Western girl.

Annette Devereaux and her father, Colonel Maximillian Devereaux, formerly of the White Pines Plantation south of Atlanta, Georgia, pulled up stakes after Sherman's troops burned their plantation and ran off most of their slaves near the end of the war. Colonel Devereaux had taken what money he could get for the land from a carpetbagger who came swarming in after the war, dug up the gold coins he had buried under the scuppernong arbor, packed his remaining goods into a wagon, and headed north to Franklin, Missouri, where he joined a wagon train headed to California by way of Santa Fe.

When she heard her father's plan to leave Georgia, Annette was surprised. She had never imagined they would leave their home and the land where her mother and baby brother were buried.

"California? But what will we do there, Papa?"

"Why, Daughter, I hear the gold nuggets are just lying on the ground in California, waiting to be picked up by anyone. We'll make our fortune back in no time, my dear. Don't you worry."

Annette looked at her father and shook her head. He had always been a dreamer, always reaching for some gold mine in the sky. It had been her mother who ran White Pines, and it was from her mother that Annette had gotten her practical nature and grasp of how to make things work. When she realized her father was determined to go west, she set him straight.

"We are not going to California to hunt for gold. There is no money in it. We need to take the money you got from selling White Pines and invest it in goods when we get there. We can go to the gold camps and sell the things the miners need—shovels, picks, denim, needles, tools, nails, you know. The demand will be high, and we can make a good profit. Then we'll buy more goods. When we find a town that looks like it will survive, we'll open a store."

Her father looked shocked. "The Devereauxs as common merchants. I won't hear of it."

"You will hear of it, Father, dear. Our old life is over. We are leaving White Pines, Mama, and all the ways of the Old South behind. Those days are gone. We have a chance to start over in a new land, where people won't judge us if we owned slaves or fought for a lost cause. If we work hard, we will survive. We have a little money, and if we are careful, we will get by."

She looked at her father sternly. "That means no expensive brandy, no white suits, and especially, no gambling."

"But, Annette, you are eliminating the only pleasures a man has."

"Papa, I think that out West you will find that a man is measured by the depth of his character and the work of his hands, not by the price of the brandy he drinks."

And so, the Devereauxs joined the Johnson train headed for Santa Fe. Max Devereaux had raised mules in Georgia, and their team was big and strong. Annette remembered the day they drove out of the torn-down gates of White Pines. The pillars that had once held the great carved arch over the wide gravel entryway were now ragged stumps, chopped down and burned for firewood by the marauding Yankees. As they left for the last time, a small group of their former slaves gathered by the roadside and wept. Jimbo, the big, powerful boss of the field crew, waved his hat and cried out.

"Why cancha tek us wif you, Marse Max? You been so good to us. What we gonna do wif freedom. We jus' fiel' hans."

Max Devereaux pulled over and reached down to take Jimbo's hand.

"You've been good, Jimbo, like family to us, but I no longer control your destiny. I can't take you with me. I only have enough for Annette and myself. You've got to make your own way now. We'll be in California. If you ever make it out there, come see us as a free man."

"Okay, Marse Max." He wiped his hand across his eyes. "Sho' gonna miss you."

Annette climbed down and embraced Sophie, the woman who had been her personal maid since she was eight years old. Sophie wept on her neck and held her close.

"You is like my own chile', Missy Annette. What will I do without you ta care fo?"

Annette wept too and kissed Sophie on the cheek. "Maybe we'll meet again, Sophie. Until then, remember that I love you."

Then Annette had climbed back on the wagon and turned her face from White Pines for the last time. Tears ran down her face, but she never looked back.

Now they were heading west. During the first part of the trip, Annette had struggled with memories, with the hardship of the journey, and with the strange food. She tried to have coffee with every meal and cook something decent, but she was a poor hand at it, having never set foot in the kitchen except to sneak apples from the big barrel in the pantry. It wasn't until Mrs. Jorgensen, one of the women in the train, took Annette under her wing that things smoothed out. Under her gracious tutelage, Annette learned how to make biscuits, fry bacon, and make a decent cup of coffee. She discovered the Dutch oven and soon was making passable stews. Annette was smart, willing, and determined to make a go of her new life. Within a month, she was well on her way and getting used to life on the trail.

The only part of the journey that bothered her were the dreams. She would awaken in the night with a horrible fear clenching her stomach. Her dreams were about that night at White Pines when those men had chased her into the barn. They were jumbled and confused, but over and over she saw the leering faces of the soldiers. They had grabbed her, torn off her bodice, and were going to ... they were going to ... And then he came. Captain Budrow. Tall, handsome, clean cut—unlike the scum who had dragged her into the stall and torn her clothing off. If there had not been a pitchfork in the stall, they would have had their way. She had seen Budrow's surprise when he came into the barn and saw what his men were up to. She saw the anger mount up in his eyes, the blood rise in his face. His hand went to his holster, he unsnapped the clasp. and took out the heavy army Colt.

"Jansen! What are you men doing? Leave that woman alone."

The one called Jansen only smirked at his captain. "This woman's ours, Captain. She's southern trash, and she deserves everything she gets. If you want to get in line, you're welcome, but if not, go find your own."

But Budrow had not backed down. "Jansen, you men are under arrest. Now drop your weapons and come with me."

Jansen had only grinned, and then his hand went for the gun in his holster. It never cleared leather as Budrow's Colt put two holes in his shirt pocket. The second man grabbed his rifle up from where it leaned against the wall and tried to get a bead on Budrow, but once again the heavy colt belched fire, and a round blue hole appeared between the man's eyes. He flopped forward on his face.

The third man threw up his hands and backed slowly away.

"Don't shoot, Captain, I ain't fighting you. You already killed my brother."

Budrow turned to her to see if Annette was all right, and the man saw his chance to run for the door. Annette had tried to cover her nakedness with her arms. Budrow picked up a horse blanket and offered it to her while averting his eyes. But their eyes had locked for just a moment, and Annette felt a rush of emotion that she had never felt before.

Budrow took Annette to her father and advised them to find a safe place to stay—away from the war and away from marauding soldiers. Max took Annette and left that evening for Savannah and the home of a friend. Annette was disturbed to hear later that Budrow had been arrested, accused of murdering the two men while they attempted to stop him from raping her. But she had been unable to go to his trial to testify on his behalf, and he had been convicted.

Now, as she sat on the wagon seat, she wondered what had happened to the handsome Union captain. He had saved her and her honor, and she prayed that something good had come of it. But in her heart, she was afraid he had been hung.

THE DRIVE

Scat Jansen rode into the small settlement outside Fort Concho, Texas. He'd come a ways since he left the army, but that didn't bother him none. He only had one thing on his mind. Find the Union captain that had gunned his brother down and kill him. The long miles behind him had only added to the obsession. He had followed Budrow all the way from Georgia. He drew up in front of the only saloon in town, slip-tied his horse and went inside, ambled to the bar, and looked at the man behind it. He wore two guns, and they were both tied down.

"Whiskey ... and bring the bottle."

"Put your money on the bar, stranger."

Scat reached down as if he was going for his wallet, but he pulled his gun and laid it alongside the bartender's head. The man sank down behind the bar without a sound, and Scat reached across and helped himself to a bottle of rye. He looked around at the men standing at the bar or sitting playing cards. He reached in his pocket and pulled out some greenbacks and laid them on the bar.

"I pay for my drinks," he said to the room, "but I don't like strangers who think I'm a deadbeat. Now any of you want a drink, come on up. I'm buying."

A few of the men walked up to the bar, but most turned back to what they were doing.

"I said, I'm buying!"

Quick as greased lightning, his gun was in his hand. "Any of you think you're too good to drink with me, make your play."

A tall man with a scar across his face from chin to ear stood up and walked over to Scat. "Okay, stranger, no offense meant. You're kinda on the prod, aren't ya? I'll drink with you if you put that gun away."

Scat slid his gun into his holster and the man picked up a glass and poured himself a drink from the bottle. A few more men helped themselves.

The tall man led Scat to a table off to the side of the room. "You here on business or pleasure, friend?"

"Business. I'm lookin' for a man. Budrow is his name. He killed my brother. I trailed him from Georgia."

"Budrow, did you say?"

"Yeah, do you know him?"

"Me and the boys had a run in with a man named Budrow out west of here a few days back. He came out on the long end of the stick. Tall man, handsome, carries a Henry rifle and a pair of Army Colts."

"That's Budrow. Do you know where he is?"

"Yeah, he was riding with a bunch of them Texas Range Rider gals. Now I hear he's trailing with Charlie Goodnight. We had a shoot-up with 'em. Budrow was there, and he killed a bunch of my men. Now I'm looking for some new riders."

"Are you going after Budrow?" Scat poured another drink from the bottle.

"Yes, sir, sure as the sun rises, we're going to catch up with them riders and skin 'em alive. Need a job?"

Scat nodded. "I'm your man. Who am I working for?"

"They call me Skin. Skin Ricketts."

CHAPTER EIGHT

ROUNDUP

Budrow pelted after three running calves and a young heifer, who were making tracks for a gully he knew he'd never get them out of unless he used a stick of dynamite. Ranger had figured out the cattle business a lot faster than Budrow and got ahead of the cow and blocked her. She bawled loudly and angrily. Budrow hoped he wouldn't have to lasso her. His last three lassos hadn't gone well. Fortunately, no one had seen how bad they'd been but Roads.

But Budrow's luck had run out. Nettie Paris shouted to him, waving her arm, yelling that he needed to lasso a steer that was heading pell-mell over a hill in his direction, chunks of mud flying from its hooves. Budrow would rather have been back at war facing the Army of Northern Virginia and all its musket and cannon fire than have Nettie gaze upon him in scorn when he did another terrible job at roping. Somewhere inside him there was a prayer.

Ranger sensed that the steer racing across the ground in front of them was their responsibility. The black gelding broke into a fast trot and then a run. Suddenly Budrow had no more time to worry about his roping deficiencies,

Nettie's scorn, or the Army of Northern Virginia. He shook out his rope as he'd seen others do and as he'd tried to do right a half-dozen times before. He had his loop, and he swung it rapidly in a circle off his right shoulder. The steer was right on top of them. *Throw, Budrow, throw!* A voice was hollering in his head. But he froze.

"THROW! You dang Yankee! THROW!"

It was Roads.

His shout, roared like an officer commanding a squad of infantrymen, made Budrow react as if he were on the field of battle. His roping arm shot forward, his fist snapped open, the lasso flashed through the air and, in a sequence that Budrow would forever compare to the parting of the Red Sea, wrapped itself around the steer's horns and snugged in tight, stopping the snorting beast in its tracks. Across the field, Nettie waved her hat in the air and shouted: "You dazzle me, Kit Budrow! Lord above, you're turning into a real Texas cowboy! Heyyyaaah!"

Was it possible his face was red? Budrow could feel the heat burning over his cheeks. Roads came up beside him on Sharpsburg and growled, "No woman wants to see a man with a red face. Cover it up, Budrow. Use the bandana around your neck. There's enough dust in the air to warrant you pulling it over your nose."

Budrow did as he was told.

"Now walk that steer over to Major Nettie Paris and get it back into the main herd. Act like it was nothing. Make no fuss over throwing a good rope."

"Understood."

"I calculate you owe me five Yankee dollars for just saving your reputation and making you shine in the eyes of a Texas beauty. You can pay me when you collect your wages at the end of the drive."

"A square deal."

"Never fear. No one heard my shout. This roundup is noisier than all the shooting and hollering and Yankee yelping at First Manassas."

Budrow moved on, drawing the steer with him. Nettie Paris waited. He figured she had a particular place she wanted him to take the animal. There was still a smile on her dusty face, burnt dark by the sun and the smile wasn't for Roads. Inside, he was all turmoil. Outside, he knew he needed to act like he'd always acted in front of his men before a battle—cool headed, in control, unafraid. But this woman. How could one woman do all this to him?

"And Budrow?"

He turned his head to look back at Roads, who was examining the crease in his hat. Roads lifted his eyes and smiled. "That was a good rope on a mean steer. We may make a cowboy out of you yet. I believe there's half a chance."

"Where's Miss Brandy Black?"

"You mean, Captain Brandy Black? I have no idea. I do not require her distraction at this present time. You, on the other hand, will have to deal with yours. She has you in her sights."

"Her sights? Nettie's LeMat looks safe in its holster."

"Ha. Her gun is the least of your worries, sir."

Budrow made his way to her. Three of Goodnight's men yeeeha'd a dozen head of cattle past him in a burst of dirt and dust. He was glad he had his mouth and nose covered. Nettie watched as he emerged from the cloud.

"You throw a dang handy rope, Kit," she said, using his nickname all by itself, her smile still fresh as morning. "Yet you say you've never cowboyed before."

"I have not."

"Then you're a quick study. Come on. Let's get your steer over to the crew holding the main herd together and then I want you to help me rustle up some strays."

"You know where they are?" Budrow asked.

"I have my suspicions."

"Just you and me?"

Her smile split open into a wide grin. "Just you and me. Is that too much for you, Kit?"

Budrow held steady. "It suits me right down to the ground, Nettie."

"Does it? We'll see."

They worked together in dry arroyos and by thin streams choked with cottonwoods. Cows and calves were hidden everywhere. They kept feeding them back into the main herd, where branding was going on, and smoke and stench was in the air. Without instructing him with words, Nettie taught him everything he needed to know about being a good cattleman by showing him. Now and then she'd catch him stealing glances at her while they worked, but she said nothing about it for a long time. Truth was, he enjoyed how she sat a horse, how she moved it and reined it in, how agile she was in the saddle. He also had to admit, as God was his witness, he liked the way her clothes fit. Finally, she reined up beside him.

"What is it?" she asked.

"What?" he responded.

"You keep looking at me."

"Just to be sure you're okay."

"Oh, I'm more than okay, Kit Budrow. What's on your mind?"

"Cattle."

She laughed. "Try again."

"I was thinking about your argument with Goodnight."

"No, you weren't. But I'll admit that is a good moment to think about."

Goodnight had cussed up and down. He would not tolerate any women working his drive. Nettie had cussed up and down that her Texas girls could outwork and outride any man and that one of her Texas Range Riders was worth five of his cowpokes. All this happened in the yard in front of Goodnight's ranch house.

"We've been guarding the border in this region all during the war," Nettie snarled. "I reckon we can handle a few cows."

"Your time is done," Goodnight had snarled back. "We're under martial law now. Soon enough, Yankee troops will be here to shut you down. Take your guns."

"I know it. But they ain't here yet, are they? We're going to ride herd with you."

"No women!"

"We were good enough to keep y'all safe during the war. We're good enough to see your herd safe out of Texas."

"I'm done arguing with you!"

Both of them were unmounted and standing on the ground. Goodnight had gestured to one of his men to get rid of Nettie. Budrow began to lower himself out of his saddle when Roads seized his arm.

"Let it be," Roads murmured.

"But I can't let one of them hurt her."

"She can take care of herself. But if one of his men draws on her, you may gun him down."

In those few seconds that he'd looked away, Nettie had handily dispatched the cowhand Goodnight had sent after her. He was flat on his back in the dirt, and Nettie was wiping the back of her arm across her mouth, ready for whatever happened next. Budrow had no idea what she'd done to him. But he saw what she did to cowpoke number two. He came at her swinging.

She dodged his first punch. Ducked his second. Then came up and plowed him in the gut with her cowhide-gloved fist. He folded, and she hammered down on his head—one, two—and he was out before he ate the dust. A third cowhand was on her and clipped her on the jaw, making her stagger. Budrow was about to launch himself from the saddle when Roads put his hand on his arm again. "Wait."

Nettie spat out blood, grinned, then waded right into the man who'd hit her, slamming him with a left, a right, a left and then when he tried to get ready for another right, she mixed it up and hit him in the head with three solid lefts in a row. The cowhand dropped like a rock.

Nettie was not afraid to brawl. I could see she was enjoying herself. Blood trickled from her mouth, her Boss of the Plains hat by J.B. Stetson was gone, her braided hair had unraveled, and she was panting as if she'd been running. But she was ready for more. In fact, it looked like she wanted more.

Goodnight stared at her, looked at the three big cowboys she'd laid out in the dirt, stared back at her as she waited, gloved hands still balled into fists, and began to laugh. It was a good, long, harsh man's belly laugh.

"You'll do." He was still laughing. "If your girls are as mule-headed as you, they'll do too. Y'all work the herd with us to the border. No farther."

Nettie had nodded and smiled, extending her hand after removing its glove. "No farther."

Goodnight had taken her hand and shaken it vigorously. He complained later it was like getting caught between the hammer and the anvil and he was surprised to get any part of his hand back from her.

"That was a time." Nettie sat her horse and looked at the blue sky. "Were you surprised at me?"

Budrow nodded. "I'm not used to seeing women fight like a man. Especially pretty women."

"Pretty women? Is that a compliment? Were you thinking of jumping down to help me?"

"I was."

"What stopped you?"

"Granite Roads."

"Did he?"

"He said you could handle yourself."

"Was he right, Kit?"

"In spades."

She was looking hard into his eyes. "Did my brawling make y'all think less of me?"

Budrow shook his head. "No."

"What did it make you think?"

"What a beautiful and powerful woman you are."

"And that doesn't frighten you away?"

"No. It ..."

He hesitated.

She waited.

He pulled his bandana down from his face. "It ... made me want you more."

Her eyes remained on his, thinking, evaluating, asking her own questions, making decisions. Finally, she leaned over from her saddle. "Make a believer out of me, Kit."

He hesitated again. But not for long. He could hear Roads in his head—*You dang fool Yankee! What are you waiting for?* He leaned towards Nettie and placed his lips on hers. A shock tore through him. Her kiss was the most amazing thing he'd ever experienced in his life. He kissed her harder. She returned his kiss with even more strength. He couldn't take being in the saddle anymore. He slid down and pulled her down with him. She was giggling because he somehow managed not to break the kiss.

Budrow drew Nettie's body as close as possible. He loved the feeling of her rugged clothing and the muscular body beneath her coat and trousers, honed like a Bowie knife by wind, sun, storms, and hard work. He couldn't get enough. It was like he was starved and his well bone dry. Her arms went around him. He loved the strength in them. They pinned him to her. She acted pretty hungry and thirsty herself.

He had no intention of breaking off until she did.

But she never pulled away and their kiss lasted seemingly forever.

CHAPTER NINE

HEADED WEST

Carson Budrow looked at the men who surrounded him. They were a tough lot of riders from every part of the west. Hardened men, many of whom had been up the trail to New Mexico the year before. Mostly Texans, there were a few Spanish vaqueros, men who sat their horses like conquistadores, a couple of Irishmen who had come along to ride ahead and set up the camps, the two lady rangers, and most interesting to Budrow, the black cowboy, Bose Ikard.

Ikard was Goodnight's shadow, carried his money, drove cows with the rest of the crew, and was a crack shot. Granite had cautioned Budrow. "That fella is a curly wolf—don't never try to back him up, because he don't take water from no man. Goodnight trusts him more than any man except Loving. He was born a slave but moved to Texas as a free man, and he is as rough and tumble as they come. But you'll never find a better man to ride the river with."

Goodnight had called his men together. The sun was just cracking over the edge of the world, and Budrow could hear the cattle milling about, wanting to move.

"Boys, this is going to be a tough haul. Last year, me and Oliver sounded out the trail, and we took cattle to Fort

Benton, New Mexico, to sell to the Army for the reservation Navajos. We went twice, and that's what staked us to this herd and this drive. Now we are going all the way to Denver. From here we head southwest to Horsehead Crossing on the Pecos River. Then we turn north and head for Colorado. We have to cross Raton Pass and pay that renegade Dick Wooten a toll. But me and Oliver scouted a new route through Trincheras Pass, and we'll be taking that next drive."

"Any Comanche up where we're going, Charlie?" one man asked.

"Yessir, you can bet on it. And beside them, there will be dust storms, lightning, prairie fires, flooded rivers, snakes, cactus, lions, and days without water. If you don't think you can handle it, quit now, and we won't think the less of you."

Budrow looked around. Not one man left. He glanced at Nettie Paris. The early morning sun rested its light on her face, her braids hung down and her flat-brimmed hat was set back above her forehead. She was listening to Goodnight and her face was lit up with excitement. Budrow had never seen a more beautiful girl ...

Well, there was Annette.

He felt a twinge of remorse. When they had been together, Nettie had not held back. When she kissed him, it was clear to Budrow she had given not only her sweet lips, but her heart. And that was confusing to him. He had never imagined he would fall for a western girl. She didn't wear dresses, her skin was bronzed, she could shoot the eye out of a lizard at two hundred yards, she rode a horse better than most men, and she could drive a herd with the best of them.

But somehow that didn't fit his picture of what his wife would be. Growing up in the east, the women he had known were soft, smelled of lilacs, and sat about in frilly white dresses, sipping tea and filling their hours with, to him, nonsensical discussions about books, recipes, and children. This western girl was none of that, and yet, in her own way, she was as feminine as any of them.

The girl he had rescued back in Georgia, Annette Devereaux, was a southern belle, white-skinned, soft, and seemingly helpless. But Budrow couldn't get a picture out of his head—the picture of Annette standing defiant against the wall of the barn with a pitchfork in her hand, the front of her dress torn away, while the Jansen brothers tried to get up the courage to rush her.

He looked away from Nettie. Granite rode up next to him.

"Somethin' troublin' you, Budrow?"

Budrow nodded toward Nettie. "Yeah, her. What am I supposed to do with her?"

Granite grinned. "If you need a lesson in that, you're not the man I thought you were."

"That's not what I mean, Roads. I mean, I'm kinda confused here. Nettie is not exactly what I had in mind for a wife."

Granite shook his head. "You still thinking about that Magnolia of the South?"

Budrow scowled and shook his head. "Yeah, but there's nothing I can do about that. I will never see Annette Devereaux again."

The herd moved west toward the crossing of the Pecos. Goodnight and Loving had mapped out the trail, and they always tried to reach water before sundown. The drovers would then put the cattle in a circle while the Irish roustabouts set up the camp. For the first several days of the drive, while the cattle were still trail-fresh, Goodnight used a double guard—half the men guarded the herd for the first part of the night and the other half for the rest of the night. If a storm threatened, everyone was on duty. After the first few weeks, the cattle had grown accustomed to the trail, and by the end of the long days, they were happy to bed down at night, so they reduced the guard to four men on each watch.

Budrow loved taking the guard in the early morning hours. The nights were growing cooler, and the dawns had a nip in the air. He would sit on Ranger or one of the other horses cut from the *remuda*, slowly circling the herd, watching as the stars above revolved around the North Star. Budrow had never seen skies so vast or stars so brilliant. When the moon rose, it cast a ghostly light on the desolate country they were passing through. The Mexican vaqueros sometimes sang to the herd—strange, wild Spanish songs of the range. This new life he found stirred him in ways he had never felt before. The ordered, small world of his boyhood was melting away, dissolving under the light of the western stars.

The long days under the blazing sun, facing the whipping wind with its dust and sand, rain and chill— all of these were doing their work on Carson Budrow. In these hours, he was shedding the polished manner of an eastern gentleman and becoming something he had never imagined—a western man.

Every day for a few minutes, Granite would work on his pistol handling.

"Remember this Budrow, it's not the man who's fastest, it's the man who shoots the straightest. Even if you get your gun out after the other hombre palms his, a lot of tinhorns shoot fast but miss. Even if you take a little lead, concentrate on making your first bullet count." Coupled with a natural coordination of eye and hand and a determination to become skilled, Budrow was soon pulling his gun and hitting his target almost as swiftly as Roads.

He was off away from the herd practicing one day, when Nettie rode up. She had an unhappy look on her face.

"Where you been, Budrow? Haven't seen much of you since we started the drive. Seems like you took the late watch to avoid me."

Budrow looked up at Nettie, sitting proudly on her horse. He felt a flush rise in his face.

"Well, I've been busy learning how to drive these cows, Nettie. Don't want to keep lookin' like the tenderfoot I am."

"Yeah, but you could at least say hello. Seems like we went a little further than just being saddle mates."

Budrow slipped his gun into his holster and looked up at her. She was lovely. Something twisted inside him.

"I've been wanting to apologize for that time, Nettie. I feel like I took advantage of you. It was not a gentlemanly thing to do."

Nettie leaned forward and looked at Budrow with her piercing blue eyes. "Apologize? For what? I wanted that just as much as you did. At least, I thought you did."

"Nettie, I ... of course I wanted it. I never knew it could be like that with a girl."

"Well then, what's the problem, buckaroo?" She looked at Budrow again. "Say, have you got another girl somewhere?"

Budrow flushed again, and his hesitation made Nettie go stiff. "You do! You lowdown skunk! Leading me on while all this time you're thinking about someone else. Why, that's the lowest ..."

"Now, Nettie, calm down. I think you're the most wonderful girl I've ..."

Nettie pulled her horse's head around. "Save that gumbo for your sweet señorita, whoever she is. It don't truck with me, Budrow. You're just another saddle bum with a handful of 'gimme' and a mouth full of 'much obliged.' I oughta shoot you where you stand. Tell you what, cowboy ..." and the word slid disparagingly from her mouth. "... Don't be coming around me no more. Keep your distance, or you'll be running with those steers out there. Get my drift, Budrow?"

She jerked the reins, and the horse leaped straight ahead. Budrow had to jump to one side, and her stirrup caught him in the ribs as she flashed by. Budrow went tumbling in the dust as Nettie rode off. Granite Roads trotted up on his big gray. There was a smile playing on his face.

"Oh, my. Looks like you set a fire under that lady's tail. What caused that?"

Budrow stood up and pulled his hat off. He used it to beat the dust out of his pants and then slammed it back on his head.

"I think I just made the biggest mistake of my life."

Annette Devereaux was tired. The wagon train had crossed into the Indian Territory north of Texas, and the days had been hot and dry. There were also rumors of Indians prowling about. Everyone in the train was on edge. Talk between father and daughter had been reduced to a few words at mealtime. Jim Chancy, their guide, had been sleeping little and watching a lot. Annette had spoken to him that morning. He was a rugged man, who had ridden the trail many times. A man of few words but plenty of action, he had been a steadfast worker and guide throughout the trip.

"Are we going to be attacked by Indians, Mr. Chancy?"

"Wal, Mizz Devereaux, that's hard to say. We're cutting through their territory, and they've been on the prod ever since the army took the Texas part of their land away. But that's not what I'm worried about."

"What, Mr. Chancy?"

"We've been trailed for the last three days. There's a band of riders with shod hosses tagging along beside us, over about five miles. Injuns don't ride shod hosses. They've been follerin' us. I cut the trail of one rider, probably their scout, yestidday." Chancy turned and spat some of the chaw that filled his cheek. "They's white men, and they is wuss than Injuns. Comancheros, we calls 'em. I reckon it's Skin Ricketts and his bunch of owlhoots. Do you have a gun, ma'am?"

Annette looked down from the wagon seat at the grizzled old scout. "Yes, Mr. Chancy, I do, a double shot derringer."

"Wal, I don't want you to worry none. I'll be taking care of you, but keep that gun right handy at all times."

"I've never shot a man, Mr. Chancy."

Chancy looked at Annette with a grim face. "If those men get in here, and you can't get away, it's not them you should be using that pistol on, Mizz Devereaux."

CHAPTER TEN

DUST

Granite Roads was riding drag. He had pulled his scarlet bandana up over his face as he followed the herd, the dry Texas land boiling up and smothering his clothes and body and turning him and his horse white. He couldn't even see who else was riding drag with him. Not that he was looking. It was enough to make sure the herd was moving ahead and no calf or cow or steer was trying to turn back.

But a shadow appeared on his right. It was hard to make out who the rider was. He watched, coaxing Sharpsburg ahead, waiting as the cowhand drew nearer. They should have stayed in their position on the other side of the herd. There must be a reason for seeking him out in this enormous cloud of dust.

"Granite."

"Major Paris." He hadn't expected it to be her. "To what do I owe this honor?"

She pulled her dust-caked scarf down from her face. "How well do you know your friend?"

Granite cringed. This was a conversation he didn't want to have. "I wouldn't call him a friend, Captain Paris. We've only known each other a few weeks. We met on the trail. Just like we met you."

"Does he have a woman?"

Granite looked at the herd. "No."

"There's a woman. I know that."

He decided to bite the bullet. "He saved her from a passel of men who wished to do her harm. They were rats, Captain Paris. Now he feels beholden to her and she to him. He saved her honor and probably her life. It has left him confused about what he ought to do next."

She was quiet a moment. The dust made her sneeze. "Where is she?"

Granite shook his head. "He has no idea."

"Has he been looking for her?"

"Not that I'm aware of. He has no idea where she is, and he hasn't been asking."

"Is he in love with her?"

"I am not an expert on Carson Budrow's inclination towards romance. But I hardly think so. He was only in her company an hour or two. Perhaps less than an hour. However, he killed for her. That has stayed lodged in his heart and mind. It makes him wonder if he should do more for her. That is the tortured thinking of a gentleman."

"He killed those men?"

"Shot them dead, yes, Captain Paris, stone dead."

"And now he's confused?"

"A gentleman's confusion."

"But you don't think it's love?"

"I think Mr. Budrow has confused honor with love. Honor is not a romance. It is a mark of courage and backbone and integrity. Love, however, is something else altogether."

"I am not going to be fair with you, Mr. Roads. I am going to ask you something point blank."

"Considering your conversation to this point, that is not surprising."

"Hang convention when my heart is at stake. I cannot drive Kit from my mind. It's most annoying. Indeed, it's infuriating. I value my independence, Mr. Roads. I don't like my feelings and freedom being roped into someone else. I don't take well to any form of dependence. Especially to a man who acts like he loves me one day and then loves another woman the next."

"Budrow does not love her."

"But he was so awkward with me the other day. Like he was hiding something."

"Any man can be permitted a certain amount of awkwardness in the presence of a beautiful and angry woman. Especially if he cannot separate one emotion from another inside his head and heart. I say again, Captain Paris, Mr. Budrow is gallant and a man of honor when it comes to the woman whose life he saved. You cannot, as a woman yourself, disrespect that. But she is not the woman he loves and adores."

"She is not?"

"She is not. As I've emphasized. As the dust and dirt roils about us."

"Speak plainly to me, sir."

Granite laughed and then coughed wildly as his mouth filled with grit. "I thought I was being plain and clear."

"No clearer than this thick cloud around you and me."

"I will say it straight then. Like a command on the battlefield. He loves you."

"He loves me?"

"Love. Yes, I say love. But the fool does not understand that. I don't know if he will understand it in a month or two months or half a year. He may yet lose you. But love, as I know love, is what is both confusing him and consuming him. And you are the object of that love."

"Do you truly believe that to be the case?"

"Without question. I see it. You ought to see it, Nettie. If I may, you would see that if you could control that towering Texas temper and pride of yours for two consecutive minutes under the Texas sun."

"Huh." She reined her horse away without another word and vanished into the milky soup that was the tail end of the cattle drive.

Granite Roads thought about everything he had said and everything Nettie Paris had said and considered he had held his own well enough. He even believed most of what he'd told her. Some had been said out of desperation. But a great deal of it had been things he'd come to understand about Budrow and his predicament as he'd talked out loud. The more he'd talked, the more Granite understood.

He had not lied to Nettie. He believed Budrow loved her. He knew Budrow better than Budrow knew Budrow. That did not necessarily mean Nettie wouldn't shoot Budrow out of the saddle one moonless night in Colorado. But she might kiss him out of the saddle too. He hoped he'd evened the odds that Budrow would get the kiss over the bullet.

"But this is Texas," he sighed out loud, pulling the bandana over his mouth and nose again. "A great deal is possible in Texas that can occur nowhere else. As God is my witness."

"Well, now I'm a witness too," a woman spoke up. "What was that all about, Granite?"

Granite looked around him.

"I'm behind you. In the dust. Where I've been for the past ten minutes." Brandy Black, masked, walked her horse up beside his. "I suppose I should have coughed or something."

"Hmm. That might have been best."

"I didn't. But I'm still confused. I thought Nettie and Kit Budrow were friends."

"Less friends than Texas lovers. Which means matters can get as cold as a blue norther or as wild as a Texas twister."

"And what about us, Granite? Am I still the gawky kid with pigtails? Or am I a woman?"

"That answer is obvious, Miss Black."

"Am I your woman?"

"Umm. I would say that question is jumping the gun, Brandy. We have a whole cattle drive ahead of us in which to resolve that issue."

"Issue? I'm an issue?" She stared at him till he looked away, still nudging Sharpsburg forward into the dirt cloud. "Do you love that Southwaite woman?"

"That I can't answer. I don't know. I don't believe I should love her."

"Why not?"

"This cattle drive is starting out as a long conversation in a mansion's drawing room. I'm not sure I'm up to it. Comanche, yes. They can descend with all the arrows and lances they wish. More incursions into the labyrinth of the human heart? I believe I need a drink."

He took note that at least she smiled, and she had not approached him with quite the cold steel that Nettie had. So, he felt free to smile back—without fearing an attack from her along the lines that he had no business smiling as if what she said to him was superficial or frivolous and didn't need to be taken seriously. He did take it seriously, but he did not have an answer for her. Not yet. In that way, he supposed, he was more like Kit Budrow than he cared to admit.

The thought was upsetting to him. He considered himself a better man than Budrow, and he liked to think of himself as decisive. Certainly, he had been decisive in battle. In his business affairs. When it came to training a horse. In a running gunfight, he was always decisive and his shots precise and lethal. Yet when it came to choosing between Ann Southwaite or Brandy Black, he had no more sense than that dang Yankee, Budrow, did when it came to making a choice between Nettie Paris and the woman he had saved in the barn in Georgia. Annette Devereaux was the name Budrow had used. They were both at a loss.

Brandy spoke up. "A nickel for your thoughts, she said to the handsome stranger."

"My thoughts?" he replied from far away, since he was lost in them.

"Yes. You've grown so quiet. What are you thinking about?"

"You," he said, which was not entirely a lie.

"Me? Just because I'm riding beside you?"

"No, my lady, I think of you a good deal when you're not around."

She arched her golden eyebrows, now coated with the thick Texas dust, and made more pronounced by the scarf that hid half her face as if it were a veil and they were both riding through an exotic land like Arabia. "Good thoughts, I hope."

"Always, Miss Black."

"Yet you cannot decide how you feel about Ann Southwaite or how you truly feel about me."

"Well ..."

"Yet I believe you feel something. And I believe that feeling is profound."

"How is it you have come to that belief, Miss Black? Has anything I've said promoted such a thought?"

"Oh, nothing you've said, sir. It is a woman's intuition. I rely on it. It is often even more accurate than words a man or woman has spoken out loud."

She reached down for the canteen that hung off her saddle horn, took a long pull from it, offered it to Roads. He hesitated, then took it and murmured his thanks. He believed he could taste her lips on the mouth of the canteen as he raised it, then returned it. He felt lightheaded, and he saw her smirk.

She knew. They both knew. She had bedeviled him. Yet he did not mind. And she knew that too. He felt her confidence about who she was to him grow with a sudden spurt. It made her sit taller in the saddle. It put strength throughout her body that was obvious in her posture and the way her legs gripped her gelding's flanks, the way her gloved hands gripped her reins. And her smile. There was this pearl of a smile on her face that arrived and would not depart. Suddenly, Roads felt like she had him in the palm of her hand, the way Ann Southwaite used to have him before the war, certain she could do whatever she wanted with him. Brandy exuded that same powerful spirit. Roads felt as if he'd been roped.

"Usually, it is men who pursue me and not I them, Granite," she said, the smile not going anywhere. "With you, it's different. It's as if I am tracking a man across the Texas plains. A fugitive. It is taking some time. It is difficult. Yet I remain confident I will overtake him. When I do, I shall best him as we wrestle in the Texas dirt. I will knock him senseless, I will get his gun and his knife, I will hogtie him. Then I'll throw him over his horse and lead both man and beast back from whence I came. He will be my prisoner for as long as I wish. I have captured him. He is mine. Do you take my meaning, Granite Roads?"

Her story shriveled him up inside. "I believe I do."

"I am a woman now, Mr. Roads. Not a child."

"I appreciate that."

"As a woman, I will see to my needs and my desires and take what I want. I will fight for them, if necessary. Do you grasp that?"

Her boldness shriveled and weakened him a bit more. "Yes."

"Then we have come a long way in our short ride together. Wouldn't you agree?"

A gust of wind dispersed the dust for a moment. They both had a clear view of the cattle drive in all its immensity and a clear view of the prairie that surrounded them, sprawling without limit from one horizon to another. They took it in, along with the enormous blue sky and a sun as golden as her hair. Which, although bound up under her Boss of the Plains hat, had worked itself loose and hung over her shoulders, just like sunlight. Impulsively, trying to find his way back to a strong, full-hearted Granite Roads, who had fought for Robert E. Lee and had a sturdy head on his shoulders, Roads whipped off his Confederate slouch hat and exclaimed, "Miss Black ... by God in heaven, you are the beauty of the Texas plains."

Her smile grew until it brightened her entire face and made her sit even more upright in the saddle. "I thank God you have come to your senses, Granite Roads. Where will we go from here?"

Roads was still not himself. Brandy had taken away part of his mind and spirit and placed them in a breast pocket of her shirt. Just as Ann Southwaite had done when he was a boy. But now, the girl who had been a girl back then had taken him where she wanted as a woman and had him in her grip, the same way she gripped her horse's reins. It was most disturbing, but he had no idea what to do next. For the first time, he wished Budrow were there to help him out. He, Granite Roads, who never needed anyone's help.

He looked straight ahead at the cattle rolling slowly along toward the Pecos River, the cowhands whistling, calling, and slapping their lassos against their saddles and keeping the herd moving. Then he leaned over towards her and took the kiss he knew she offered. It was a long kiss, and it made his mind whirl like a twister. He wanted more. She gave him more. It felt like the last link in a chain she was fashioning. He didn't care.

If this was love, then true love wasn't so unpleasant after all. He was confident he'd figure it all out and gain back the upper hand with Brandy Black. But when he lifted his lips away and looked at her face and the strength in her perpetual smile, he knew she still had the upper hand and all the aces in the deck, and no intention of relinquishing them to him.

CHAPTER ELEVEN

HORSEHEAD CROSSING

Rain! Indians! Dust storms! And nasty, mossy-horned killer Texas Longhorns. Longhorns that wanted to either run at the slightest provocation or turn on the drovers and kill them.

I guess I've died and gone to hell.

Carson Budrow sat by the fire waiting for coffee. He had never been a coffee drinker, but out here on the wretched east Texas plains it was the very fluid of life. Johnny Sutton, one of the hands, sat down on the log next to Budrow and handed him a cup. It was burning hot and black as night, but Budrow gulped it down.

They had been moving the herd through torrential rainstorms, every thunderclap an excuse for the ten thousand head of cattle to light a shuck into the desert. Budrow grew tough under the constant toil, his hips narrowing and his shoulders broadening. The land the herd was traveling through was some of the most desolate Budrow had ever seen, Grey alkali flats, rocky outcrops with not a bit of green and worst of all, no water. What fell during the frequent downpours was sucked up by the dry, sandy soil or rushed away down washes and gullies toward the Pecos.

A few days before they got to the Pecos, Old Man Charlie Goodnight sent Loving on ahead to scout the trail, and they hadn't heard from him yet. On the third day of Loving's absence, Goodnight walked up to the fire and called his drivers around.

"We're comin' to the Pecos, boys, and believe me, it's the most desolate country you will ever see, the graveyard of the cowman's hopes. When a wicked man dies, he either goes to hell or God sends him down to the Pecos."

And Budrow agreed. This was the most God-forsaken country he had ever seen. The cattle had not tasted water for three days, and they were jumpy and nervous.

Goodnight went on. "I haven't heard from Oliver about what's ahead, so I don't know if the Comanche are waiting for us, if the river is at flood stage, or what, so I don't know what to expect. We'll be coming on the river tomorrow, and you fellers have to do everything you can to keep the cows from running when they smell the water. Stay in front of them and keep them from bolting if you can. But if they go, jump that bronc out of the way quick or there won't be enough left of you to send home to your folks. If it's at flood stage and they run into it, we'll lose a lot of cows."

Johnny grinned. "Maybe Ol' Blue can keep the rest of them from jumpin'. He's the best lead steer I ever seen."

Budrow shook his head. "Ol' Blue may be smart, but he's still a cow, and if he gets a scent of that water, he'll run too."

Just then there was the clatter of hooves, and a rider came busting into camp. It was "One-Armed" Bill Wilson. He jumped off his horse and strode up to Goodnight. There was a bloody bandage around his arm.

"What happened, Bill?"

Bill took off his hat and dusted it off on his chaps. "Comanche. We got jumped at the bend about twenty miles up the river. Oliver got shot. He's okay. We hooked up with some Mex traders, and they're taking him on to Fort Sumner. He sent me back to warn you. Pecos is in flood, and the Comanche are around, and they're on the prod."

Goodnight grinned. "Well, boys, this is what we come for. We're gonna get those cows across that river come hell or high water. Who's with me?"

Several rebel yells split the night. "We're with you, Charlie!"

The next day, everyone was up early. They got the cattle up and moving down a road that ran through a wilderness of stone and cactus, greasewood trees and gray earth. Though there was some grass, the thirsty cattle did not graze but sniffed the air, looking for the tiniest scent of water. Before the sun rose, clouds rolled in and obscured it. The gloomy canopy overhead fitted the strange, desolate country, and Budrow, riding out to the side of the herd, felt an icy chill that wasn't just the bitter wind. They were approaching a rise and Goodnight rode by.

"The river's just over that hill. There's also some gullies and arroyos where the Comanches could hide so keep sharp boys." He rode on past.

Just then Budrow heard a horse running up behind and turning, saw Nettie Paris coming at a gallop. She pulled the reins, swung in beside him and grinned.

"Gonna be some hard ridin' in a bit, Budrow. You better stick with me."

"I thought you were gonna shoot me the next time you saw me, Nettie."

"Wal, I reckon I was hasty on that, Kit."

Budrow looked at Nettie. "Only my friends call me Kit."

She moved her horse closer. "Look, Budrow. I had a little chat with Roads, and he gave me a few tips. So, I figure I pretty much know what's going on with you. I'm a woman who, when she sets her sights, most often hits what she's aiming at."

Budrow stopped his horse and looked at Nettie. "Did Roads tell you my secret?"

Nettie looked puzzled. "What's your secret?"

"Well, I figure if we're gonna make this work, you should know everything about me."

"What's to know? Out here in the west, his actions, not his past, judge a man."

"You sure about that, Nettie?"

She cocked her head and looked at him. "What's going on, Kit?"

"I rode for the Union. I was at Gettysburg, like I told you, but I was in Hancock's corps, not Jeb Stuart's."

Nettie's face paled. "You're a ... a Yankee?"

Budrow nodded his head. "Yep, fought through the entire war in blue."

"But you and Granite ... you're pards, ain't you?"

"Working on it, Nettie. I'll be his pard if he'll have me. Granite saved me from a bunch of renegades that were fixin' to hang me for my pants and steal my horse. He ran them off and we've been ridin' together since then."

"But a ... a damn Yankee?" Nettie's face grew hard. "That just about fries the beans, Budrow. And to think I was getting all ready to put my brand on you. Why you low-down ..."

Just then, there was the sound of a shot and then a volley. Bose Ikard galloped by.

"Injuns, trying to stampede the cattle. Stay sharp boys!"

THE DRIVE

The heads of the herd jerked up, and the cattle moved. A breeze sprang up, and even Budrow could smell the water. The gunshots and the scent of water broke the herd, and they began to run. Up over the rise, Budrow galloped his horse, trying to get ahead of the herd to turn them. Below him, pale sunlight broke through the clouds to shine upon a winding silver river that in its curving formed a bend in the shape of a horse's head. It flowed out of a grey and green wilderness. Goodnight and several of the men charged the Comanches and found that it was only a small party, looking to get a few beeves for food. Budrow saw them riding off up a wash headed south with a few riders in pursuit.

The foremost cattle had reached the river, which was running strong. They were wild for water. The ones behind pushed the leaders right into the river. Thirst-crazed longhorns fell beneath the hooves of their herd mates, drowned in the swirling water or caught in quicksand along the bank. The main part of the herd was still running down the hill. Budrow and Nettie were trying to turn them, when Nettie's horse put its foot into a hole and went down. Nettie pitched over the head of the horse and landed on her face. Several yards away, Budrow saw her struggling to get up as she looked up at the cattle charging down on her. He could see her mouth form his name. "Kit." But he couldn't hear her over the noise of the herd.

He had never spurred Ranger, but this time he dug his rowels in, and Ranger leaped like a deer. He rode down on Nettie, who sprang up and lifted her arms. Leaning down over his pommel, he grabbed her outstretched hands, and she swung up behind him. He pulled Ranger up so hard that he almost sat down on his haunches. The big horse saw the cattle thundering down on them a few yards away, and turning on a dime, raced toward the edge of the herd.

He had to push his way through a few head, but the press was gone, and they forced their way out into the clear.

Budrow jumped down and pulled Nettie off the horse. She clung to him with a grip like steel. "Nettie, Nettie are you okay? Are you all right?"

"Kit, oh Kit, ya saved me." She buried her face in his shoulder and he could feel sobs shaking her body.

"Nettie, darlin'." His arms went around her, and she lifted her tear-streaked face.

"Am I, Kit? Am I?"

"What, Nettie?"

"Am I your darlin'?"

"Yes, Nettie. And I'm gonna hold you to what you said."

"What, Kit, what?"

"You said that out west a man is known by his deeds and not by his past. I want that. This land is changing me, Nettie. I feel more alive than I ever have. And now that I've found you, the past, what I was, what I did ... well, it matters no more. All I know is that I've got a new lease on life, and I want to live it to the fullest. And I want you to live it with me."

Nettie put her head on his shoulder, and for the first time, the toughness and bravado left her voice. The Nettie that spoke was all woman, soft, feminine, his woman.

"All right, Kit, if that's what you want, I'm in for the distance," she whispered. "I'm gonna ride for the Budrow brand if you'll have me."

They were silent for a moment, and then she looked up and grinned. "My personal damn Yankee."

The crew spent three days of recuperating at Horsehead Crossing—a bone-littered ford that the Kiowas and Comanches had used for many years during their annual raiding parties into Mexico. They spent much of the time dragging steers out of mudholes, searching the brakes for strays, and getting the herd back together. Big diamondback rattlers infested the hills around the crossing, and Budrow got lots of pistol practice shooting snakes.

Finally, they moved the herd out and headed north on the first cattle drive from Texas to Colorado. They crossed the river again to the eastern side, north of Horsehead, and headed for Pope's Crossing on the Texas-New Mexico line.

At Pope's Crossing, the night before they crossed the border, Charlie called Granite, Brandy, Budrow, and Nettie to the fire. They were expecting to be reminded that the girls could only ride with them to the Texas line. Charlie pulled out some makin's and built a smoke. "They're called cigarettes," he grinned. "I learnt it from the Mexican vaqueros." Then he looked at the girls. "You girls said you would turn back at the Texas border, and I planned to hold you to your word."

Nettie looked at Budrow with a scowl. Brandy started to say something.

Charlie raised his hand. "Now just hold your horses, ladies. Gimme a chance to speak my piece." He took a long drag. "You both been excellent hands, better than some. You're tough, you work hard, and you're a big help. And with them Comanches on the prod, I can't in good conscience send you back. So, I've decided. I'm gonna let you finish the drive."

Budrow grinned, and Granite shook Charlie's hand. "That's mighty good of you, Charlie, mighty good."

"Well, don't do anything to make me change my mind," he said gruffly and walked away.

The next morning, as the sun rose, they moved the herd back over to the western side of the river to more favorable terrain. They were in New Mexico.

CHAPTER TWELVE

ROUGHNECKS

"I'll whip you for the no-good Yankee you are!"

A crack snapped through Granite Roads's ears and made him jerk up his head.

He had been dozing in the saddle as he worked the west side of the drive that was snaking north towards Colorado.

A dream image of Brandy Black dissolved, her smile still vivid, her words soft: "I'd like to marry you, my handsome man, and be your blushing bride."

Another crack.

"Let me see what kinda blood you got, Northern boy. Let me see you bleed."

Roads saw a bullwhip slash the air about a hundred yards away.

Saw Kit Budrow's arm raised to protect his face.

Saw the sleeve of his jacket and his shirt were ripped and torn.

Saw that Goodnight and Loving were practically out of sight and definitely out of earshot at the head of the herd.

Saw that Bose Ikard was even farther ahead than they were.

Saw Brandy Black and Nettie Paris were up and gone to the east of the cattle, rounding up a half-dozen strays.

Roads took all this in between the second and third whip strikes.

He spurred his horse.

His Navy Six was in his hand.

Budrow had wrapped a bleeding hand around one of the whips and yanked the cowboy out of the saddle with a powerful jerk. But when he took the time to do that, another cowboy Roads recognized as a skunk Goodnight had hired against his advice named Grill Sabbat, slashed his bullwhip across Budrow's back. Budrow arched his back in pain. Sabbat laughed and drew back for another cut, aiming for Budrow's face.

The next crack was Roads's revolver.

It was the worst kind of shot to make—a pistol on a small target taken at full gallop and head on. The ball went high and shattered Sabbat's elbow. He yelled in pain and dropped the whip with a loud curse. Roads shrugged as he and Sharpsburg galloped on. "You understand getting y'all to drop the whip was my intention."

Roads never stopped the gallop.

It was a cavalry charge, and by heaven and all that was holy, his Civil War saber was strapped to his saddle.

He let out an ear-splitting rebel howl, drew the saber and smacked Sabbat with it. The man flew off his horse in a spurt of blood.

Roads had left the saber in its scabbard. Otherwise, Grill Sabbat would have become the headless horseman.

Not a bad idea.

He saw another cowboy pointing a LeMat at him. He knew he could not get off the first shot. But a rifle barrel was suddenly pressed into the cowboy's skull.

"Lose it, Shimrock!" barked the rifleman. "Or I'll smash you like a bowl of eggs!"

"But he's a stinking bluebelly, Conrad."

"I was at Appomattox, Shimrock. Grant treated us right. Let us keep our horses and arms. The Yanks gave us rations. Water. I never forgot that. I'll go to the devil before I'll let you shoot this man in cold blood."

"I got others backing my play, Conrad. Look behind you."

"They are the ones that ought to be looking." It was Bose Ikard's deep, gravelly voice. He was sitting his horse, a horse all lathered from a fast run, and covering everyone with a fat sawed-off shotgun. "Next man moves, gets a gut full of lead balls. Big ones."

Roads sat still in the saddle, sheathed saber across his knees.

"What's going on?" Bose demanded.

"He's a no-good Yankee!" one man shouted.

"Likely rode with Sherman!" bellowed another.

"We ought to string him up and let him dance!" This from Shimrock, who had lowered his LeMat but still had Conrad's rifle barrel rammed against the side of his head.

"We gotta kill him." Sabbat was on his feet, his nose swollen, bloody, and clearly broken by Roads's sheathed saber, his right arm dangling and useless because of Roads's shot. "That's the only right thing to do."

"The war's over," spat Conrad.

"The heck it is," snarled Sabbat. "It ain't never gonna be over."

"Even Nathan Bedford Forrest allowed it was done, and only a fool would think otherwise," said Conrad.

"Then Forrest was the fool."

Without a thought, Roads raised his Navy Six. "Take it back."

"By God's heaven, I won't."

Roads cocked his revolver. "What you said about Forrest? Take it back. I rode with him some. I'll give y'all a three count, you weasel."

Bose cocked both barrels of his shotgun. "That's enough bickering. Easy does it, Granite. You rebel lowlifes might recall the war set me free. Free to shoot you dead and ride away. Mr. Goodnight hired Budrow. He's on the payroll. He's been a hard worker. He stays with the drive all the way to Denver."

"Straight as Jehovah's gun barrel he does." Goodnight had ridden up. "But you buckaroos—Sabbat, Shimrock, Bilder—with your big mouths I heard half a mile away, clear out. I got no further use for you. Draw the wages you got owing from Bose and go back to your holes in Texas. Go now."

"You can't do that!" squawked Shimrock, the rifle barrel still pretty much in his ear. "I need that money for a grubstake!"

"He can and did," rumbled Bose, pointing the shotgun at him. "Get on the move."

"I won't! I'll sue!"

There was a roar of hooves.

Nettie and Brandy pounded up.

Bose rolled his eyes, lowered his shotgun, and shook his head at Sabbat. "I ain't helping you out here."

Nettie took it all in and screeched when she saw Budrow spattered in blood. "Who did this to you?"

"Nettie—" Budrow tried to begin.

"WHO?"

One-armed Sabbat spat blood and phlegm. "I did. And by all that's good and holy, I'll do it again!"

Bose grunted. "Poor choice of words."

Nettie leaped from her horse, punched Sabbat in the face with her gloved right fist, hit him again with her left fist, also tightly gloved, dealt him another right and another left, each blow making him stagger like he'd been shot, plowed a left into his gut, then drove her knee hard into his head and nose. Sabbat screamed, and she reached back to Texas with a final left and hammered him. He dropped and didn't move.

Nettie stood over his body with her fists balled. "That was sweet as sugar. I want you to get up so's I can enjoy beating the living tar out of you all over again."

Before anyone could react, Bilder, a big, well-muscled man, jumped Nettie from his horse, knocked her flat, shoved her face into the dirt and began to whale on her with his huge ham-sized fists.

Roads was about to make a similar leap from his horse onto Bilder when Brandy swooped in with her lasso, snared Bilder, hauled him off Nettie, then rode a couple of hundred yards off, dragging him, then dragged him back at a furious pace. Bilder tried to struggle to his feet. Brandy sprang down in front of everyone, booted Bilder in the ribs full out and sent him sprawling, pounced, straddled the big man, and began pounding him with her fists.

Her blows came so fast that Roads lost count. After a minute or two, she hauled a battered Bilder to his feet, choking him by the collar to make him stand straight and started slapping him hard across the face with her right hand. Left and right, left and right, till blood splashed from his lips and nose, and he spat out a tooth. Then she decked him with one huge right. Like Sabbat, he dropped like a rock. She crammed her boot into his face and didn't care if her spur cut him up or not.

"I'd make you lick it, you brute," she hissed, "if only I'd thought to stop beating you into seven kinds of pork so you'd still be awake to get the boots put to ya."

Roads smiled. He had scarcely believed it when he'd heard Brandy had beaten up two men in a bar fight while he'd been off to war, killed a third in a brawl in a barn, shot God knows how many outlaws, and bested four men in four separate knife fights using her Bowie, one fatally. Then he realized, once again, watching her demolish Big Joe Bilder, that she had been a Range Rider for some five years and outmuscled and outhustled countless desperadoes on the Texas frontier using her firearms, her wits, her Bowie, and her bare hands. She was smaller than Nettie, even prettier in a genteel sort of way, but no less tough or rugged or, to put it more directly, manly. He watched her kick dirt over Bilder's face, her cheeks still red with fire and fury. She was a bona fide tomboy.

Goodnight was laughing. "If that don't beat all. I guess the gals on our crew really are worth four or five men put together. There was some talk of sending you two back after we were safely over the Pecos with the herd. But the argument was put that you'd be only two against a Comanche attack. Now I see I can't spare you. Sabbat and Shimrock and Bilder—or what the ladies left of them— are heading back to Texas on a rail in the half-hour, and I can't lose my two cowgirls to boot. I reckon our Texas roughnecks will be with us all the way to Denver. How does that suit you, Miss Paris? Miss Black?"

Nettie was back on her feet. She and Brandy exchanged a look. Nettie nodded. "That suits us just fine, sir."

"It's settled." Goodnight swept his eyes over the cowhands clustered there. "The war's over, boys. Time to swallow or spit your plug. No more of this. You have a chance to get good money if we bring this herd into Denver and we don't run all the fat off them. A stake to help you all build a new life. Don't throw it away like these fools just done." He glared at Shimrock, the only one of the three not flat in the dirt. "Git. I don't want to see any of you again." He reined his horse away. "You can take that rifle off his head, Conrad."

Brandy smiled up at Roads. Her face was speckled with blood like a plover's egg, but it wasn't hers. Her silver hair was in disarray too, and her gloves were red with the gush she'd cracked from Big Joe Bilder's veins. "You want to change your mind, Granite? I must look a sight."

Roads smiled back. He was still holding his sheathed sword across his lap. "Oh, you are a sight all right."

"I'm not your plantation belle. You saw what I can do. I'm more than hoop skirts and mint juleps."

"I like that."

"Do you? There was a time I might have been more like a lady. Then the war came, the men left, and I learned to be a lawman and a gunslinger."

"And something of a pugilist," he added.

"I had no choice, Granite," she argued. "I had to learn to defend myself."

"I know. I do not disparage it. I admire it."

"Are you sure?"

"You think I do not find you feminine?" Granite took off his gray slouch hat and ran a hand through his thick, dark hair. "I find you are very much a woman. Beautiful with poise, courage, grace."

She shook her head, biting her lip. "Oh, I don't know anymore."

"I shall prove it to you. Once we arrive in Denver, we must dine together at the most elegant location available."

She laughed. "Are you sure there are any?"

"I will find them. I shall see you dressed in silks and pearls."

"Oh my, you are a dreamer, Granite Roads."

"At your service, ma'am." He swept his hat.

Her face soured. "Did you just call me ma'am?"

"A mere slip of the tongue. I meant to call you wildcat."

She laughed. Her laughter saved the moment for Roads.

He glanced back, looking for Budrow.

"Nettie is caring for him," Brandy said, following his eyes. "He'll be more than all right. That Yankee may have occasion yet to thank Grill Sabbat for whipping him, given Nettie's tender affections."

"He may indeed. Perhaps I should have been whipped too."

Claret took his meaning and let a she-devil grin slip over her face. "Y'all don't need to wish for that, sir. I'll give you a kiss instead."

Roads put his slouch hat back on his head. "A hero's reward, Miss Black."

CHAPTER THIRTEEN

AMBUSH

Annette Devereaux sat quietly on the seat next to her father as the wagon moved through the canyon. The walls rose almost straight up. They had been traveling through a rugged country, and Jim Chancy was pushing them hard. They had stopped at a waterhole at sundown and rested their animals for a few hours. While they rested, Annette sat in the stillness. She was tired and wanted to sleep, but as she sat, she became aware of the desert things around her, things that she had grown to love, though she knew not why.

The wind in the desert has a sound of its own, and that sound can be different among rocks, greasewood, or whispering through the Joshua trees or cactus. She had learned to tell the difference between the rustling of small animals, the fall of rocks displaced by the alternating heat of the day, and the cold of the night. A stone may fall, a trickle of sand may follow, then silence. She had learned that a rock moved by a foot has a distinct sound—different than a falling rock—sharper, more definite.

Annette had grown to love this desolate land, for it reached something in her spirit that she had never experienced before. It seemed the desert was always waiting, vast, immeasurable. The seeds that fall on the sand wait patiently for the first rain, and then the desolate sands break forth to leaf out, bloom, and drop blossoms and leaves in a matter of days. She waited now in the moonlight, feeling something in her heart, a voice, an emptiness, a stillness.

Her thoughts turned to the handsome officer who had rescued her. Where was he now? Did he even remember that day? She knew so little about him. He had brought her safely to her father that night and told him he must leave now, get away, get to a safe place.

Was he still alive? Did they hang him? By the time they got back to White Pines, the war was over, the Union army gone, and no one could tell her about Budrow.

The night was clear, and the moon was just rising when Chancy rousted the travelers and told them to get hitched up.

"I want to get a jump on the varmints that's trailing us. They're probably sitting around their campfire, and we can steal a march on them. I want to get through the canyon ahead before they get wise that we have moved."

Now, they were rumbling down the trail through a cleft in one of the small ranges that rose out of the grey desert. Jim Chancy rode by, a serious frown on his face. Annette saw he was looking everywhere.

"Keep your eyes open, Mizz Devereaux, this is a fine place for an attack."

"How far to Santa Fe, Mister Chancy?"

"Wal, I reckon we're about six days traveling. We'll get over to New Mexico tomorrow. We're crossing the top of the Chihuahua desert right now, runs all the way down into central Mexico." He spit a wad of tobacco. "You still got that pistol, Mizz Devereaux?"

Annette felt the reassuring bulk of the pistol in her belt. "Yes, Jim, I have it right here."

"Good. You remember what I told you. Ya don't want to fall into the hands of them Comancheros. I think the crew that's follerin' us is Skin Ricketts and his boys. He's the worst of a terrible lot."

Chancy rode ahead. The trail turned to the right and descended back to the playa, where the flat desert spread before them. At the mouth of the small canyon, a few rocks stood up in the desert, silent sentinels to the passing of many westward-bound immigrants. The wagons crept past them, seeking the safety of the next settlement down the road.

Suddenly, the rocks ahead erupted in flashes of light— she saw them before she heard the rifles. She saw Chancy's horse go down with the first fusillade, and then her father jerked beside her and tumbled off the wagon seat.

"Father! Father!"

She jumped down and went to him. His head was covered in blood, and he was limp and lifeless. As she stood up to cry for help, she saw several horsemen break from the other side of the canyon and come racing up around the wagons, blasting fire into the men driving them. Two of them rode her down as she reached for her pistol and she went down, stunned by the impact of the horse's charge, as her pistol flew into the dark. She tried to raise herself, but one horseman leaped off his animal and knocked her down with a blow of his fist. Then he jerked her to her feet.

"Well, well, well. What do we have here? Seems like I seen you before, missy."

Annette was looking into the twisted face from her nightmare. It was one of the men from that night at White

Pines, but how ... how could that be? That was in Georgia, and this is in the far west. A sickening grin passed over the man's face as he stared at her.

"Don't have a pitchfork now, do ya, little lady?"

The gunshots in the background had subsided to a few here and there as the gunmen finished off the survivors. The rest were busy looting the wagons. A tall man with a narrow, scarred face strode up beside her captor.

"What do we have here, Jansen? A little treat for the men?"

Scat Jansen whirled on Skin Ricketts. "This here belle of the old south is the reason my brother and my cousin is daid. I got unfinished business with her. When I'm done, you can have what's left."

Annette stared. It was him, Jansen, the one who got away. But how, how could this be? "You're Jansen. You were there that night."

"That's right, missy. I was there, and now I'm here. And guess what? Your boyfriend is right down the trail, not a day's ride from here."

"Captain Budrow? Here?"

"Yep. And now I got you, maybe I can get him too."

He walked over to Max. "Hey, old man, can you hear me."

Max stirred and opened his eyes. "Yes, I can hear you."

Jansen grinned. "I'm leaving you alive, old man, for one reason. Tomorrow, some cowboys are coming through here, and my old partner, Captain Carson Budrow, is riding with 'em. I want you to give him a message."

Max nodded.

"Tell him, I got his sweetheart, and if he wants her, come and find me."

He kicked the old man in the side. Max cried out.

"Father, Father," Annette cried, trying to go to him. Jansen jerked her back.

"You're lucky he ain't dead. But pretty soon you're gonna wish you was."

Jansen grinned and then struck Annette again with his fist. She felt her legs go limp and then the darkness fell ...

The New Mexico morning came with a chill wind. Budrow and Granite had risen early, finished their coffee, and were now riding point, the chuck wagon rolling off to the left. Behind them, the cattle moved slowly with Ol' Blue in the lead. Granite pulled his horse to a halt and lifted his head.

"What's up, Granite?"

"I smell smoke, but it ain't prairie fire smoke—it's wood smoke. It's comin' downwind, so it's over north a ways." He pointed.

Budrow followed where Granite was pointing and moved his eyes along the horizon. There! A faint wisp of smoke at the base of one of the small mountain ranges that cut the land.

"I reckon we best ride over and see, Budrow."

Budrow whistled to Goodnight and pointed toward the smoke, and signaled that he and Granite were going to see what was up. Ranger fell into an easy lope, and Granite followed right behind on his grey. As they drew closer, they could see that the smoke was rising from a bunch of wagons in a line. The wagons had come out of the mouth of a canyon that split the hill. The two men rode in. The scene was horrific. Men and women lay sprawled where they had been shot down. Goods, bedding, and furniture were scattered on the ground. There were no horses or mules. They had all been unhitched and Budrow could see the trail of many animals leading off to the northwest.

"Indians?"

Granite shook his head and pointed at the tracks. "Iron-shod horses. No Indian would ride one unless he stole it. And the bodies haven't been mutilated. No, these were white men, Comancheros, and they were in a hurry."

Out of the corner of his eye, Budrow saw a movement behind a bush. He signaled Granite, and the two men drew their pistols and fanned out to each side.

Granite called out. "We're coming in with our guns out, and if you want to start the ball, we'll dance right along with you."

A weak voice called out. "Who are you?"

"Trail riders with Charlie Goodnight, bringing a herd up Colorado way. We ain't Comancheros."

"Come on in then, we need help here."

Budrow moved in on the right, and Granite came left. Behind the bush, they found two men. One was propped up against a tree. Blood stained the front of his shirt. He had an older white-haired man next to him. The old man's face was covered with blood from what looked like a head wound, and his white shirt was red with blood as well. They didn't look good.

"Ya got any water? We been here all night, shot to rag dolls without a sip."

Granite snaked his pistol into his holster and fetched his canteen. He handed it to the younger man.

"Go easy, just a few sips at first."

The man took a sip and let it soak into his dried-out mouth. Then he lifted the head of the older man and helped him to take a drink.

"What happened here?" Budrow asked.

"Comancheros is what happened. Skin Ricketts and his murdering crew."

Budrow ripped a piece of the old man's shirt off, soaked it in water from his canteen and began washing his face clear of blood. As the blood washed away, he looked down in shock.

"I know this man."

The old man's eyes opened, and he looked up at Budrow. "Hello, Captain."

"Mr. Devereaux! What are you doing here?"

The other man looked at Budrow with amazement. "You know Max?"

Max groaned and took hold of Budrow's arm. "They got her, Captain, they got my Annette. That man's got her. You have to fetch her."

Budrow looked at Granite. "Get the wagon over here, we gotta get these men some help."

Granite jumped on his horse and headed toward the herd. In a few minutes, Budrow saw the dust trailing out behind the wagon as it raced toward them.

"Who are you? And what's this about Annette?" Budrow asked the younger man.

"I'm Jim Chancy. I was ramrodding this train. Mr. Devereaux and his daughter Annette joined up in Missouri. We were doing fine, but then I cut the trail of some men who were tailing us. I tried to keep everybody on the alert. I was expecting them to jump us when we were draggin' up the pass. But they didn't, and I thought we was in the clear when we started down the hill."

"Then Ricketts jumped us when we came out of the canyon. Shot me out of the saddle on the first go round. Shot Max down too. I played dead under my horse until they left. They killed everyone and robbed the wagons of money, guns, and ammunition. They brutalized some women before they killed them. It was terrible, and then one of them, I heard her call him Jansen, dragged Annette away and put her on a horse. I heard him say something about knowing you."

Budrow felt a shock go through him.

Jansen! How in the world did he get here?

That night, they held a powwow around the fire. Jim Chancy was there, his arm in a sling and looking pale. Bose Ikard came over, got some coffee, and sat down. "The old man is okay. He's got a nasty bullet burn on his scalp and a fairly superficial wound in his side. He looked a lot worse than he was because of all the blood, but he's gonna make it."

Budrow looked around. "What about Annette? We can't leave her with those men."

Chancy shook his head. "Women prisoners don't live long when Ricketts gets 'em. I think you just give her up."

Budrow shook his head. "Scat Jansen isn't going to kill Annette—he's going to make her suffer first. You see, I rescued Annette from Jansen and his brother back at the end of the war. I killed his brother and his cousin. He's got a big grudge against her and me. Somehow, he knows I'm trailing with Charlie here. Ricketts probably told him about our dust up north of the Canadian. Now he wants me to rescue her again. But this time he'll be ready."

One-armed Bill spit a chaw and then spoke. "The part of Colorado you're headed into is rugged. I don't see how you can find them, Budrow."

Nettie, who was sitting just outside the circle of the firelight, spoke up. "Cain't leave her with Ricketts, Budrow. You gotta fetch her."

"But, Nettie ..."

"Gotta go, Kit, and I'm going with you. I got three friends buried back at Granite's ranch because of Ricketts."

Granite looked up. "I'm going too, Kit …"

Budrow looked at Granite in surprise. "You never called me Kit before."

Granite grinned and shrugged.

Another voice chimed in. It was Brandy. "I'm goin' too, Budrow. Let's see if those side winding polecats can handle the four of us."

Charlie Goodnight looked grim. "I gotta get this herd to Colorado. That's gonna take another week. I'm gonna hold 'em at Apishapa Canyon, bring some more up and then move on to Denver. When I get to the ranch, I got plenty of boys that will help fetch you out, if you get stuck. If I don't hear from you in ten days, we're coming after you."

Budrow turned to Nettie. "You sure about this, Nettie?"

"Kit, you're my man. I don't want no ghosts between us."

CHAPTER FOURTEEN

THE HUNT

Roads allowed he had not expected tracking to be another rabbit that Brandy Black pulled out of her bag of tricks. He realized he was still adjusting to a girl who had been in pigtails in 1861, when he left for war, and who was now a woman, six years older, pigtails long gone, and competent at any number of tasks he would have thought only men could be good at. He watched her scout the way they should go, keeping fifty to sixty yards ahead, leading her horse by the reins, eyes to the hardscrabble ground. Roads glanced at Nettie Paris, whose eyes shone with pride as she watched Brandy drop to her knees to examine a hoof print.

"We found out how good she was back in '63," Nettie told him. "A bunch of stone killers had eluded us for weeks—burning out ranches, stealing horses, slaughtering everyone in their path, even putting babies at the breast in the grave. It was intolerable. It made me crazy. But we kept losing their trail. Like they were phantoms. Till one day, Brandy asked if she could try. Lord, she was still so young. Her woman's beauty had not yet arrived. She was gawky and unkempt and pure tomboy. So much tomboy that she made a lot of young men look weak and unmanly. But we were at sixes and sevens so far as those killers went, so I told her to go ahead a hundred yards in all directions and see what she could spot. I'll be danged if that ugly duckling didn't pick up a sign we'd all missed after only ten minutes of poking around. It was faint, but it was there, and it was for sure the plug-uglies we wanted to skin alive. In two days, Brandy took us right to their door, a cave in a riverbed not even a Comanche would have spotted without a brass scope and an eagle's eyes."

"And I'll tell you what, Granite Roads. I made it clear she was to come back for us and not to take on those owlhoots on her own. I'll be danged if the only reason I knew she had tracked 'em down was the sound of shooting. We went like sheet lightning for where the gunfire was popping and found her peppering the cave with her Henry rifle. She said she'd told 'em to come out, that she was the law, they'd fired at her, and that was it. She put paid to all four of those killers. I think ricochets took half of 'em. We dragged out their bodies, and two of the polecats had bullets in their heads, in their backs, in their legs, and in their chests. She looked at them and didn't even flinch. And that's four years back now. That's how young she was. She says to me, 'Major, baby killers don't deserve jail, another swallow of water, or any kind of hot meal. We oughtn't to waste good rope on them. Lead is sufficient. If I could've, I'd just have used my fists or a knife.'"

"So, now, here she is, tracking another mess of snakes. I see you still worry about her, Granite, and that's a sweetness in your disposition. I don't mind it at all. Just makes you manly in a woman's eyes. That goes for your pal Kit too. A gentle man who holds back his rough ways until they are truly required is the fullness of manhood so far as I am concerned. But do not misjudge Miss Black anymore, Granite. If there is a person in my life who has been the epitome of an avenging angel, it is she. Pity the ones she turns her sights on. I'd have thought you'd have figured that out by now. Especially after the whaling she laid on the sidewinder that jumped me when I was pounding the man who bullwhipped Kit. You would not credit your eyes with the things I've seen her do to wicked men. She breaks them in half with her bare hands or slits them neck to toes with her Bowie. And it is a real Alamo Bowie, sir. By James Black, who made the one Jim Bowie used to split Santa Anna's soldiers in twain. I know there is almighty controversy about who made the first Bowies, but I go with Black. And Brandy's has a date stamp on the blade by the hilt, the only one like it I've seen–1836, the year Bowie was killed along with Crockett and all the others, God bless 'em."

Roads nodded. He didn't mind when Nettie rambled. Tracking was dull work. "Any relation between James Black and Brandy's family?"

"Not that I know of. But I doubt Brandy's ever looked into it. There's been no time."

"How did she come by it?"

"Why, she took it off an owlhoot she killed up by that little town of Dallas. Claimed it as her rightful prize. She's used it to dispatch many a desperado since. That would have been '64, as my memory serves. Doesn't that terrorize you more than Tecumseh Sherman a-marchin' through Georgia? Are you sure you want to tame that pretty-eyed hellion?"

Roads smiled and looked down at the cigarette he was fixing for himself, rolling the tobacco up in the white paper he had removed from the front of a Yankee Bible. "I don't think I'll ever tame her any more than I could tame a wild catamount. I have no intentions of doing so. I'll take her just the way she is … if she'll have me."

"Why, that little girl can rob Granite Roads of his strength and confidence?"

Roads lit his cigarette and smoked it happily, looking up at the sun. "A beautiful woman has a lot of power, Nettie. You ought to know it, considering how beautiful you are. Pistols and artillery can't do the damage a bewitching woman can."

"I know what I can do to a man, Granite." Nettie smirked her devil girl smirk. "Yes, Miss Black is a great beauty now. She turns heads everywhere she goes. I have heard rumors that a Comanche chief wants her for his bride and plans to abduct her. You see? She drives all manner of men to their knees. So, I am not surprised to see she has done the same to the great war hero of the Texas Confederacy."

"Hmm." Granite was wreathed in white smoke, but it could not diminish the sharp gleam in his eye. "I wonder if that Comanche chief hasn't pondered waking up with his own knife in his belly and her long gone while he dies a slow death."

"What makes you think you might not wake up that way one morning?"

"Because I will love her, Nettie. I will love her and serve her with a love she has never known. You are mistaken if you think it is just her fine looks that draw me in on her golden lasso. Her spirit attracts me the most. By heaven, I admire her sand and the passionate fire inside her. She is bigger than Texas. I would not change a thing. Even when she was a girl of fourteen or fifteen, and I a young buck of eighteen or nineteen who thought war would be an adventure, I admired her feisty spirit. I still do."

"Was war an adventure?" Nettie asked quietly.

"It was not. But Brandy Black is."

There were several nights without a fire as they

tracked Skin Ricketts and the fugitives west. Brandy felt the outlaws had stopped trying to make time and were looking for a place to hole up. One night, she told Granite she felt they were very close, and she had to make sure their group didn't ride past them.

Granite listened. He held a coffee in one hand and gently played with Brandy's silver-blonde hair with the other. She let him. Even leaned into him and rested her head on his chest. Nettie saw them as she curled up in Budrow's arms. She told Granite the next morning she had never seen Brandy let any man play with her hair. Texas cowboys had come and Texas cowboys had gone, but Brandy had never let anyone touch her like that.

"She likes you something fierce, Granite," Nettie said as she swung into the saddle for another day's tracking. "Don't make a hot mess out of it."

Brandy led them deeper and deeper into rough and tumble country. The weather did not hold. Budrow saw the funnel clouds first. He shouted a warning. Roads could not believe it. He had heard tell of twisters in New Mexico, but he had never countenanced it. Now he saw one cloud touch the earth with its sharp tip.

"That arroyo there!" yelled Nettie. "Everyone! Now!"

Roads saw Brandy hesitate.

"Brandy!" he hollered. "Move!"

"But I'll lose the sign!" she argued as the wind began to scream. "The storm will wipe it out, and we'll lose them!"

"We'll pick it up again! Wait much longer and you'll lose your life!"

"I can't!"

He galloped over to her and swatted her horse's flank as hard as he could with the flat of his hand. "I can!"

The horse bolted, racing after the other horses onto a trail that led down into the dry riverbed.

Brandy turned to say something to Roads, furious, when the wind threw a thick chunk of wood into her head. She fell off her horse as if she'd been shot. Roads jumped down, scooped her up, and ran deeper into the arroyo. Finally, he dropped behind a boulder, sheltering her with his body, dabbing at her cut with his bandana and water from the canteen at his hip. He glanced up and saw the others were flat on the ground, their horses with them. Budrow had his and Roads's horse's reins. Dust choked the air.

The shrieking grew louder as the twister approached. Roads knew twisters were unpredictable. The one bearing down could suck them out of the riverbed and hurl them and their horses half a mile away and break their necks in the bargain. Or veer off and cause no damage at all. Precious little could be done. It would be over quickly, and they'd be dead or alive. He had a few moments to think about how he might have lived his life differently since he'd left home six years before. Then it was dark, and the wind was a howling beast with the sharpest teeth.

As loud as the twister was, Roads still heard someone praying. How was that possible? Yet the words were unmistakable. *Yea, though I walk through the valley of the shadow of death, I will fear no evil, for thou art with me.* Startled by the closeness of the voice, he glanced down. It was Brandy.

Her eyes remained closed, but she continued to recite the psalm, her lips moving slowly. Her bleeding had stopped. Roads reached down to touch the wound with his fingers. Her hand reached up, took his, and held it close to her lips. She kissed his fingers.

"Thank you," she said, though the screech of the twister stole the words away.

But Roads could read her lips. He bent down and

kissed her hair and her forehead. Then the wind dropped. Faster and faster and faster till in ten minutes there was nothing. Slowly, they got up. Women and men and horses were coated in gray dust. No one was hurt.

Budrow led the way out of the riverbed, the reins of his horse and Roads's horse in his hands, Ranger and Sharpsburg. The others followed. Roads helped Brandy walk out. She hung onto him as she squinted at the sun and blue sky and stared at the land that rolled north and west towards Colorado and Denver.

"They had to go to ground just like us," Brandy said, spitting out some dirt. "They ain't scooting across this hard country as fast as they can. They want us to do that. Then come at us from behind. Their tracks are gone, but I don't need their tracks anymore." She turned to Nettie and smiled, cracking the dust over her mouth and face. "I know where they are, Major Paris."

Nettie raised two dusty eyebrows. "Do you now? And where is that?"

"Do y'all remember that place called Brown's Hole?"

CHAPTER FIFTEEN

SHOWDOWN

Budrow and Granite sat on their horses and looked down at the opening to the canyon below them. They were high on a ridge hidden in a large stand of Aspen, so they weren't skylined on top of the ridge so that someone below might spot them.

Granite pointed. "That there is the Gates of Lodore. A wanderin' mountain man named it that because it reminded him of Robert Southey's poem, 'The Cataracts of Lodore.'"

The canyon walls narrowed between two hogback ridges and a smooth brownish green river flowed lazily out of the mouth into the valley behind them.

Budrow trailed his eyes along the canyon walls, looking for anyone stationed as a lookout. "You been here before, Roads?"

"Yep, a long time ago. My pa and I rode here with Kit Carson before the war. Seems a lot of folks who were comin' out to California for the gold rush stopped here for wintering range. They built shacks and dugouts to winter in, and some stayed and built ranches. The outlaws moved in with them, and since then there's been a mix of ranchers, cowboys, outlaws, and homesteaders livin' here. The ranchers tolerate the outlaws as long as they don't rustle any of their cattle."

Budrow took off his hat and wiped his brow. "That entrance looks like a good defensive spot where a few men could hold off a sizeable force."

"That it is, Budrow, but there's another way in."

Granite pointed up the hill. "See where that draw opens up? Well, there's a trail there. Not much of a trail. I think it was an old one the Utes used when they lived in here. Carson showed it to me when I was a kid. He found it in 1845, the first time he came to Brown's Hole. It'll take us right up on top without being seen and then about two miles down there's a slide we can work down. If we're careful, we'll get in there with nobody seeing us."

Brandy moved up beside them. "Yeah, but how to we find where they've got her?"

"I guess we just look around."

Brandy shook her head. "We don't have time. There's only one way."

Budrow looked at her. "What way?"

Brandy grinned. "I've tracked Skin this far. I just follow those tracks in. When I find him. I meet you at the slide, and then, we go get her."

Granite shook his head. "That ain't gonna happen, girl. Too much risk. You tellin' me you're just gonna waltz past the guards?"

"Not exactly waltz, Granite. Not everybody in Brown's Hole is an outlaw. There's a bunch of ranchers in there, too, and I know some of them. If I get stopped, I'll just tell them I'm going to see Willie Kennedy and his wife, Ann. Then I'll just follow Skin's trail until I find them. Someone in that bunch has a horse with a cracked shoe on the off hoof. Might as well put up a sign every hundred feet saying, 'Here I am, follow me.'"

"You sure, Brandy?"

"Piece of cake, Roads." Brandy smiled sweetly. "Why? Don't you want nothin' to befall your poor, weak little gal?"

Granite smiled back. "With you following them, it's Skin Ricketts and his pards that I'm worried about. Plus, I want some of this action, and you might just follow them into their camp and shoot it out with them before we get there."

Brandy shook her head. "I'm gonna need a little help. There's too many of them. I'd get some, but they might get me too."

"Okay, I'll go with it 'cause it will save us some time. But I don't like it much."

Budrow looked at Granite. "So, what's the plan?"

Roads nodded up at the draw. "You, me, and Nettie will head up over the top around dusk. Brandy follows the tracks in now, and when she locates the camp, she heads over to the slide and waits for us to come down. Then we ride in, get the drop on them, and fetch Annette out."

"How many of them are there?"

Granite hooked his leg around the pommel of his saddle, pulled out the makin's and built a smoke. "Brandy says twelve horses, so that would be eleven men plus Annette, maybe less if some animals are pack horses."

Budrow shook his head. "That's, at least, three for each of us. So, what if one of them starts the ball?"

Granite grinned. "We dance with 'em."

Nettie reached into the scabbard on her saddle and pulled out a strange looking rifle. "This here's an 1855 Colt revolving shotgun. One-armed Bill gave it to me as an equalizer. We get in close, and I guarantee you when those owlhoots see this beauty, there won't be no dancin' at all."

Brandy rode down the trail along the river into the canyon. As she was passing an outcrop of rocks, a man stepped out with a rifle. "Goin' somewhere, stranger?" The man stepped closer, and then his eyes widened with surprise.

Brandy smiled. "See somethin' you like, cowboy?"

"Wal, I should smile, I do. What's a purty little thing like you doin' ridin' into Brown's Hole?"

"I'm comin' to see Willie Kennedy and his wife. Ann's my cousin. Didn't think I'd meet a big, handsome man like you, though."

"Well, why don't you just step down here, missy, and I'll show you what a big handsome man like me does with a woman like you."

Brandy swung down off her horse. The guard stepped a little closer, a salacious grin spreading on his face. He cradled his rifle in his arms. Then he stopped and squinted suspiciously at Brandy as a thought came to him. "Where'd you come from, missy?"

Brandy tilted her head coquettishly. "Texas."

"You tellin' me that a little gal like you rode all the way here from Texas by yerself?"

Suddenly, the Colt revolver that had been in Brandy's holster was in her hand, pointed right at the guard's midsection. "Nope, not by myself. I brought a friend. Now drop the rifle and turn around."

The man laid his rifle down and turned around. The next thing he felt was the barrel of Brandy's colt laid against the side of his head rather forcefully. After that, Brandy surmised that he felt nothing. She dragged him into the hollow behind the rock where he'd been sitting, and with a couple of piggin' strings, she tied his hands and feet. Then she stuffed his bandana into his mouth. "You stay there and be a good fellow. And maybe this experience will help you to learn better manners."

Brandy swung up into her saddle and rode off down the trail, following the horse with the broken shoe.

At dusk, Granite, Budrow, and Nettie sat at the top of the slide that led down into the valley. Granite pointed along the edge of the slide. "There's a trail there. We need to get down before it gets dark. Let your horse find the way. We don't want any big rocks rollin' down, or any people for that matter."

Granite put his horse to the trail, and the big gray, a mountain-born horse, went right over. Nettie followed, and Budrow brought up the rear. Ranger balked for a minute, but seeing the other horses go ahead calmed him, and he followed along. Budrow could tell he was nervous. He patted the horse's neck.

"Don't worry, Ranger. I don't like it any more than you do."

The horses went down the trail quietly, and by sundown, the three riders were at the bottom of the wall. They sat on their horses in a clump of cedar trees, waiting for Brandy. Just as the last golden rays went down over the far edge of the canyon, they heard the strike of an iron-shod horse on a rock below. Granite moved his horse to the edge of the trees and looked down. Then he nodded to Budrow and Nettie.

"It's Brandy."

They moved out and down the hill, keeping to the shadows. Brandy rode up.

"They're not far. They've got a camp with a small cabin. I counted nine horses in the corral, and I saw eight men. There's another one takin' a nap down the canyon a ways. I didn't see the girl, so most likely she's in the cabin, and maybe one man is in there with her.

"Jansen," said Budrow.

Brandy nodded. "There's a door in the back of the cabin, so one of us could get inside and get the drop on whoever's in there."

Budrow looked at Granite. "So, what's the plan?"

Granite pulled his gun and made sure it was loaded. "Budrow, you go around and get into the cabin. When you bring out the girl, we'll ride up kinda friendly-like and stand 'em up. Then we run off their horses and hightail it."

"That's a plan?"

"You got a better one?"

Budrow shook his head. "Not exactly."

"Okay, then. Let's go."

The outlaw cabin was set in a hollow surrounded by trees, which gave excellent cover to the four of them. Leaving Ranger with the other three, who waited in the shadows at the edge of the clearing, Budrow got down and worked his way through the woods until he came up behind the cabin. Moving quietly, he stepped up on the porch and moved quickly to the open window. Inside, he saw a familiar sight. Scat Jansen moving toward Annette Devereaux, who was backed up against the wall. But this time, she had no pitchfork.

"Well, girlie, I've been waiting a long time for this."

"Keep away from me, you beast," Annette hissed.

"Not likely. You're gonna pay for my brother and my cousin. Then when I'm done, I'll give what's left of ya to the fellers out there. They been a long time without women."

Budrow stepped through the door with his gun drawn.

"Just never learn, do you, Jansen?"

The outlaw whirled and went for his gun but thought better of it when he saw Budrow not five feet away with his gun pointed right at his belly and a finger to his lips. His hand stopped as quickly as it had gone into action.

"If you want to live and not get gut-shot, you'll drop that gun and put your hands up."

A startled gasp broke from Annette's lips. "Captain Budrow! What ..."

"We'll talk later, Miss Devereaux. Right now, we got to get you out of here. Now drop it, Jansen, or skin that smoke wagon and go to work."

Jansen dropped it.

Budrow motioned for Jansen to walk ahead. Annette stepped behind him and they went out the door.

"Howdy, boys. Nice night for dyin' don't you think?"

The outlaws jerked to their feet and whirled around. Some started for their guns.

"I wouldn't do that, fellers." Granite and the two rangers rode into the light behind them. Nettie had her shotgun out.

"Nettie here has a revolving shotgun with four loads. Since you fellers are all bunched up, she could probably do four of you at once, and then she has three more shots. Now, how many of you want to die? Because if you start the ball, a lot of you will, starting with you, Skin." Granite's rifle swung, so it was pointed straight at Skin Ricketts's chest.

Budrow walked Jansen out of the cabin with Annette close behind. Granite noticed two of the men edging toward the shadows. "Step back into the light, boys."

Suddenly, one man went for his gun. Another one joined in. Budrow slammed his gun down on Jansen's head and he crumpled in a heap. Then he shot the man closest to him in the throat. Nettie's shotgun roared, and two more men went down. Meanwhile, Granite and Brandy shot the two men going for their guns before they cleared leather. The rest of the men raised their hands. "Don't shoot, mister, don't shoot no more. We're done."

Granite moved his horse closer. "Good, now throw down your weapons right here. Then get down on your faces."

The outlaws complied. Budrow looked around. "Where's Ricketts?"

Nettie looked around. "He musta slipped away. Just like that yeller dog to run out on his boys."

Budrow looked behind him. Jansen was gone too!

Granite pointed at the corral. "Budrow, run their horses out of there but save one for Annette, that black with the saddle on him."

Budrow ran to the corral, and taking the reins of the saddled horse, he opened the gate and fired his pistol. The horses scrambled out and headed for the woods.

Budrow turned to Annette. "Are you all right?"

"Well, Captain Budrow, I'm fine ... now. It seems like you're my guardian angel." Then a shadow crossed her face. "Jansen killed my father."

"No, ma'am, your father's still alive. We came upon the burned-out wagons and found Mr. Chancy and your father hiding out in some rocks. They are both just fine."

"Oh, Captain Budrow, that is such good news. How can I ever thank you?" Annette threw her arms around Budrow.

"You can thank him by getting up on that horse and ridin' outta here with us before the rest of the owlhoots in this valley come down on us with guns a'blazin."

Annette looked up into the cool eyes of Nettie Paris.

CHAPTER SIXTEEN

OVER THE MOON

The sky was endless, as endless as the land beneath it. Different from Texas and yet some things brought home closer. Roads hung back from the others, including Brandy, took out his Bible paper, and placed good Virginia tobacco in it. He had trouble getting his cigarette lit even though there was no wind. Finally, he could get smoke and inhale. He smiled. Tobacco pleased him. He had used a pipe, but a bullet shattered it at Petersburg. There were plans in his head to replace it. Smoking helped him think clearly.

Roads kept his eyes on the others as they made their way to Goodnight's ranch. He watched for sun sparkling on steel in the rough scrabble rock around them. Shapes that were not the shapes of boulders or brush or dirt. His ears detected the wingbeats of flies, he'd been told. The curtain had risen on a good deal of drama during their cattle drive. Thankfully, today was not like that. He blew out another stream of smoke and was content.

His eyes picked up Budrow. He had been riding alongside Nettie. Now he was alongside Annette. In due time, he'd make his way back to Roads, waffling once more. Roads shook his head. Perhaps the day would have drama and theater yet. Budrow had proven himself a good Yankee in a fight, if there could be such a thing as a cussed good Yankee. But with women? It might be he would never prove to be decisive.

Roads smoked, walked Sharpsburg, and waited. Nettie had not shot Budrow yet, so that was a minor accomplishment on his part.

In ten minutes, Budrow was beside him.

"Granite, I ..."

Roads held up his hand with the cigarette in it. "Withhold for a moment, good Kit. First, a jigger of whiskey. Then a draw on my cigarette here. Then, I tell you before God, a verse from the Good Book."

"Granite, I can't ..."

"I swear, Kit, we do not use that word here." Roads produced a brass flask that had CSA engraved on it. "Take a Yankee swallow. I trust it will approach a shot I'd pour you in San Antone."

Budrow took a swig and coughed. Roads handed him the cigarette. Budrow hesitated.

"Take it," Roads said. "No scruples here. Just smoke."

Budrow did and coughed some more.

Roads took back his cigarette and placed it between his lips. Then he leaned over and tugged a worn black leather Bible from his saddlebag. He smiled at the surprise scrawled on Budrow's face.

"David and Samson were not genteel men," Roads said. "Neither were Moses, Elijah, nor Peter, for that matter."

He flipped through the pages until he found what he wanted and recited. "'There be three things which are too wonderful for me, yea, four which I know not: the way of an eagle in the air, the way of a serpent upon a rock, the way of a ship in the midst of the sea, and the way of a man with a maid.' The Book of Proverbs."

Roads tucked the Bible back in his saddlebag.

Budrow waited.

"Is there a sermon with this?" he asked.

Roads blew smoke. "There ought to be."

"Why?"

"Because, sir, I cannot leave you with 'there be three things which are too wonderful for me, yea, four which I know not.' You had better know, and you had better know soon."

"Know what?"

"Do not dance with me, Budrow," Roads growled. "My card is full. You know precisely what. You must cross the Rubicon. The line in the sand drawn."

"You confuse me," Budrow complained.

Roads heaved a sigh as far as Colorado. "Your lack of knowledge of military history and anecdote is appalling. I will speak plainly, sir. Annette or Nettie Paris. You have to know. You cannot declare for one of them on a Sunday and then for the other the following Tuesday. I have told you before. To save a woman's life is a good thing, but it does not mean you must marry her as if she carries your child. You are not beholden to her, nor she to you. No scruples, sir. Where does your passion lie? If you had not saved her life, how would she sit in your heart this hour?"

Budrow did not respond.

Roads pointed at him with his cigarette, which was now half gone. "Do not dally with Nettie's affections. She knows you saved Annette's life. She knows there is bound to be a bond because of that. But she will not tolerate your indecisiveness forever. I'm surprised she has not seen fit to blow your fool Yankee head clean off long before this." Roads puffed. "Is this how you brought us up short at Sharpsburg? This dilly-dallying about? Decide on your action and then bring it to pass. And that as soon as you can. Or, I do swear it before God, you will lose them both."

Roads did not see that anything was resolved over the next few days, any more than any aspect of Budrow's romances had been resolved over the duration of the cattle drive. He did, however, take note that Budrow, for the most part, rode alone. Not unlike Roads himself, who, though he enjoyed Brandy's company, also enjoyed his solitude and the freedom to commune with God Almighty's splendid creation.

What pleased him about the new track Budrow was following was the Yankee had ceased to drift between Annette and Nettie. He spoke to them at meals or when they all relaxed around the night fire. But he was not hanging by a thread on either of them. Perhaps he was actually thinking about what he felt for both and how it differed from one woman to the other. That would be a welcome transition from his muddled thinking of many weeks' duration. Too many weeks.

Roads did not dwell on it much. He brooded over Skin Ricketts far more. That sidewinder might show up at any time. A ne'er-do-well who enjoyed killing like some men enjoyed their morning coffee. The first they might realize he was stalking them was a bullet in someone's head. Maybe Budrow's. But maybe Roads's own. If he appeared half asleep in the saddle to some, it was an illusion. He heard what others did not, noticed what others missed, sensed what no one else was aware of. And his right hand always rested on his hip by his Navy Six.

Nights he did often slip away with Brandy. Her heavenly scent mingled with the scent of the land and the scrub brush and whatever scent constellations might put off that was misread and misunderstood. The world they rode in baked by day and exuded its spirit at night, a perfume finer than anything from Paris or Florence. Brandy's was a wondrous concoction of the scent of her skin, as it cooled from the day, the honest sweat no bandana sprinkled by a canteen could ever fully remove, and the fire trapped in her thick, silver hair. The heat of her scent pricked Roads's nostrils and filled him with its warmth as it touched fingers to him, his head in her lap. Her glorious lap. No better moon ever looked down at him than the silver that framed her face and eyes.

"What do you think about when you gaze at me like that, Mr. Roads?" she teased.

"Why, not just one thing, Miss Black."

"Tell me. You have to tell me."

"I think how annoying we find the dust, so that we cover our mouths and noses from it, yet when it settles on you, I do not mind it at all."

"Well, I mind it. I do not find it romantic."

"Ah, because you cannot see yourself. Right now, it's like stardust."

She rolled her eyes. "Oh, Granite, your smooth tongue. It is not."

He placed his hand on his heart. "I swear."

She traced a pattern on his forehead. He could not discern its shape or meaning.

"What else do you see when you look at me?" Brandy asked, continuing to move her finger.

"Strength. Wisdom—so much wisdom in one so young. A toughness like cannon steel, virtually unbreakable. But then this amazing beauty. Fast and swift and radiant, shining like a shooting star."

"If it's so fast and so swift, how can you see it?"

"You can spot a shooting star, can't you?" he murmured. "This is the same."

"But then it's over and gone." She snapped her fingers. A night bird stirred at the sharp pop. "Is that me? Over and gone?"

Roads laughed quietly. "How you do twist my words. You ought to take up law or divinity. There is a difference between you and a shooting star, Brandy."

"Oh? And what is that?"

"You exist on earth. You have ground under your feet and air in your lungs. Such stars as you have constellations in your eyes. You have the flash and the fire of the falling star, but the difference is you are earthbound, and you last. My love, you are quite simply a miracle."

He knew she liked his compliments. Yet it was in her tomboy nature to refuse to luxuriate in them. She had to maintain her independence. So, she pushed his gallantries away, even though she was the one who coaxed them forth. She did not wish to be told she would be pretty in a frilly dress if she donned one in Denver. She might spit if he said that to her or look away in disgust. Yet she still wanted Roads to tell her she would be pretty in a frilly dress if she donned one in Denver. Such was the charming and irresistible conundrum and complexity that was the beautiful Brandy Black.

And it was on such a night, where they lay together on a colorful Mexican blanket behind a scramble of rocks, not speaking a word, that they heard two people settle down on the other side, and Carson Budrow say, "I've thought this through."

"I believe you." They heard Nettie's voice.

"For a long time, I felt I must do more because I saved her life."

"I know it. I understand that."

"Now, I feel I've given her enough. I can't give her anything more. That's over and done. It's you, Nettie. I want to give everything to you. All that I have."

"What the heck are you saying, Kit? Have you been spending too much time with Granite Roads and his silver tongue?"

"I've hardly spoken to him in a week."

"Then talk plainly to me. I may be hardscrabble, but I'm still a woman. Tell me what you want."

"You, Nettie. I want to marry you. I have nothing to tell you past that. I'm over the moon in love with you."

CHAPTER SEVENTEEN

WOLVES ON THE PROWL

Scat Jansen picked up the bottle and poured himself another drink. Ricketts sat across the small table and grinned at him. They were in The Silver Dollar Saloon in Cloud City, a booming mining town outside of Denver. Drunken miners in hobnailed boots and cowboys wearing tied-down guns on their hips lined the bar. Thin-faced card sharks in black, broadcloth coats and flat-brimmed hats sat at tables around the room, looking for the easy pickin's that their skilled but not-so-honest hands could bring them. Hard-faced girls in revealing outfits circulated, looking for a free drink or someone interested in a visit to a room upstairs. A tinny honky-tonk piano added to the general din.

Scat was sweating from consumption of red likker. The bandage around his head where Budrow had walloped him made his plastered-down hair look even more ghoulish. He swallowed the drink and poured another. Then he slammed his fist down on the table.

"I'm gonna kill that Budrow if it's the last thing I do. And I'm gonna have that woman."

Ricketts shook his head. "There are plenty of women around, Scat. Why do you want her, in particular?"

"You just don't understand, do ya, Skin? I'm Tennessee born. We Jansens are feuders. Budrow killed my brother *and* my cousin. I can't rest until he pays the debt. And it will be paid when I'm standin' over the cold, daid body of Captain Carson Budrow."

"But why the woman?"

Jansen took another drink. "She's the cause of it all. If she coulda just accommodated me and my brother, there woulda been no problems. But she had to fight, to preserve her honor. What she didn't get was them rebels are all trash, her included. We won, they lost, so we burned them out, tore down their plantations, and hung the men from the nearest tree. The women we reserved for other purposes until we was done with 'em. To us, there was no difference between her and the slaves she kept. All them southerners was human scum. She deserves to die. But not before I gets my way."

Ricketts looked at Jansen and grinned again. He shook his head slowly as he took a drink.

Funny how this man is callin' other folks human scum.

Jansen almost shouted. "So, are you with me, Ricketts, or do I go my own way?"

Skin laughed. "Okay, okay, Jansen, just don't get yourself all het up. You've been a pretty good saddle pard, and you pulled me out of hot water when we did that bank job down in Abilene."

"You bet I pulled you out of hot water. That bank teller come up from behind the counter with a loaded shotgun. You didn't even see him. If I hadn't turned around and shot him full of holes, you'd be pushin' up daisies in the Boot Hill outside of that town. You owe me."

"Okay, Jansen, okay. I'll go with you. But only on condition of share and share alike with the woman. You get Budrow, but I get Roads." He took another drink. "You got a plan?"

Jansen shook his head. "I ain't thunk it through that far."

Ricketts leaned forward, shaking his head. "I didn't think so. So, here's my plan. Goodnight has a winter ranch down at Apishaba Canyon. My boys been scoutin' it and listening in a local saloon. Some of Goodnight's boys get a little loose tongued when you feed them red likker. That girl is there, all right, and it seems like he's also got rid of his stock ranch in New Mexico, and he's buyin' straight from Chisolm. He's got a herd down there that needs to be driv' up here. A bunch of his boys are goin' down to get it. That will leave the ranch short-handed and the herd unprotected. What say we go down there, get the girl and run off some of that herd. And if Budrow and Granite Roads are there, we'll kill 'em. How's that sound?"

Jansen took another drink and stuck out his hand. "Sounds like a plan, pard. Shake on it."

Nettie Paris stood by the corral at Goodnight's ranch in Apishaba Canyon and watched her dark-haired rival work the stallion. It was obvious that Annette knew what she was doing, for the big black horse had a reputation as a man-breaker and yet the girl had sweet-talked him into behaving nicely and taking a bit.

Nettie turned to Brandy. "Danged good horsewoman for a Georgia peach. She's got that bronc eatin' out of her hand." She climbed up on the rail and sat watching. Finally, she hollered at Annette. "Where'd you learn to handle horses, gal?"

Annette led the black to the railing and looked up. "My father owned the finest racehorses in the south— thoroughbreds all—and they were much more, shall we say, nervous, than this boy. High-strung and ready to jump. We had a great trainer, and he taught me all he knew. I ... I insisted."

Brandy climbed up beside Nettie. "The prerogative of being the spoiled daughter of a rich planter?"

Annette didn't back down an inch. "Spoiled maybe, horsewoman, absolutely. I hear that nobody has ridden this stallion yet."

Nettie nodded. "That's right, he's a man-killer, so they say."

Annette smiled sweetly. "Well, I'm no man." She patted the black on the neck and he nuzzled her hand. "What will you give me if I ride him?"

"Shootin' lessons?"

Annette smiled again. "Exactly what I had in mind. If a gal is gonna survive in the west, she has to handle a gun."

"From what I hear, yer pretty good with a pitchfork. Might not need a gun." Nettie smiled sweetly back.

Annette's face flamed. "Did Captain Budrow tell you that?"

"Well, yes. It was kind of a confession."

Brandy turned her head away and chuckled.

"A confession?"

"Well, yes, you see he had never seen a woman, well, you know, close up and personal, and he felt he had to tell someone."

"So, he told you!"

"Well, we are engaged."

Brandy was trying her best not to burst out laughing. "I guess ... I guess he didn't want to die with his sin on his head."

Annette looked at Nettie and then at Brandy. Her face grew hard like flint, and the red turned to white. Her eyes flashed, and she lifted her head. "You two think you're pretty hot stuff, with your roping and branding and shooting and your smart-mouth talking. Well, I'm just as much a woman as either of you, and I'll prove it."

She grabbed the horse's mane and swung up on his back like an Indian. "And when he gets back from New Mexico, you can tell your big-mouth boyfriend he can go to blazes."

Annette jerked the reins hard. The big stallion snorted, reared up on his back legs, and then whirled and bolted for the far side of the corral. Annette pulled his head up and he jumped right up over the top pole like a bird. He hit the ground in full gallop and then he headed down the lane, running like the wind.

Nettie stared after the shrinking figure. "Little high-strung, don't ya think?"

Brandy nodded and shook her head. "I think she got her dander up, for sure. Wal, we better go chase her down before she gets too far away."

Nettie grinned. "Aww, let her work it off. I think she was hopin' to work her way back into Budrow's affections. When I told her we were engaged, her chin kinda dropped."

"Well, you could've gone a little easier on her. That was kind of a delicate situation Budrow found her in."

"Well, Brandy, this is how I see it. He rescued her twice. Anyone who saves another person's life feels a connection. And the one who got saved feels the same. And it's even closer if a man saves a woman's life. I know a guy, a straight shooter, who brought an owlhoot he found in a big snowstorm down the mountain. The man's horse had fallen, and the rustler broke his leg. My friend should have left him there. The man was a rustler and a drunk, but my friend did the right thing and brought him out. Well, when the outlaw got out of prison, he rode out to my friend's ranch, told him he'd gone straight, and asked him for a job. My friend took him on, and they became best friends. Now that old rustler is the top hand on that ranch and one of the best cattlemen in the west."

"And your point is?"

"I don't want our little Southern belle thinking that just because Budrow saved her twice, they can become best friends."

Brandy laughed out loud. "Yeah, and move out to your ranch and ride for the brand?"

Nettie swatted her friend. "That, my dear Brandy, will never happen."

Skin Ricketts put his glass down and crawled backwards down the short slope to where Jansen was waiting. "Well, Jansen, it don't look like they sent all their riders off to New Mexico after all. That herd down there has a lot of riders around it. I saw One-armed Bill and some other of those old curly wolves from Texas. And I didn't see Budrow or Roads. So, two parts of our plan is shot to blazes."

"What do you reckon we should do, Skin?"

"Well, I say we take our boys and ride. Up at the head of the valley, there's some breaks and there have to be a lot of cows with calves up in there. While the main herd is down at the other end, we'll do a quick comb through and get us a couple hundred head. At forty a head, that's eight thousand dollars. Not bad for a day's work."

Jansen spit from his chaw. "Where do we sell them?"

"I got a buyer back in Cloud City that don't ask questions and has some fellers working for him that are mighty good with hot wire and a runnin' iron. They can turn Goodnight's brand into something completely different.

Only way you could tell after these boys get through is to skin the cow and turn the hide inside out."

Jansen spit again, the brown tobacco adding to the other elements in his scruffy beard. "Sounds good."

Skin mounted his horse and then looked back toward the ranch. He turned the horse and gazed toward the ranch compound.

"Wadda 'ya see, Skin?"

"Well, Scat, you old coyote. It looks like you may get your wish after all. Take a look."

Ricketts handed Jansen the glass. Jansen saw a horse coming down the road, running full out. "So, it's a horse."

"Look closer at who's riding it."

Jansen took another look. Then he turned to Ricketts and grinned. "Well, well, well. That girl just can't seem to stay out of trouble."

"Nope, and she's coming right past us. You get off that side and I'll stay behind this brush, and we'll hold her up. Got yer rope?"

Jansen nodded.

Annette was going full out down the road. The black loved to run, and she had given him his head, but after a mile or so, she reined him back to a trot. As she passed a large outcropping of rocks, a rope whistled out and snugged around her arms. The rope went taut, and it jerked her from the horse. She hit the ground hard. With the wind knocked out of her, she lay gasping on the ground. The black trotted off and then turned back to see what had happened. Annette opened her eyes and looked up. The grinning face of Scat Jansen leered back down at her.

"Well, well. If it isn't my little Georgia peach. You know, darlin', it just seems like the Good Lord fated us to be together. Now get up!"

Jansen jerked Annette to her knees and then stood her up. Ricketts tried to grab the black, but he backed away, and then dodged into the brush. Jansen pulled the rope off, and then grabbed Annette and tried to kiss her, but she slapped him hard.

Jansen started to knock her down, but Ricketts stopped his hand.

"We want her unspoiled. She is our bait to get Roads and Budrow. Granite will come after those cows, and if I don't miss my bet, Budrow will come after the gal. After we kill them, she's all yours."

Jansen backed off. "What'll we do about her horse? He's took off. And how will they know we got her?"

"They got Brandy Black, the best tracker east of the Pecos. She'll cut our sign sure enough and lead 'em right to Cloud City. As for the girl, put her up on your horse, Jansen. We'll get another horse from the boys. Then we'll get those cows and get back to Cloud City. If I'm not mistaken, we'll have visitors soon, but it'll be on our ground with our men around."

Jansen heaved Annette up on the horse and quickly tied her hands behind her back with a piggin' string. The two men took off up the valley road.

After a while, the big black came back out of the brush and looked down the road after Annette. Then he snorted and headed back toward the ranch.

CHAPTER EIGHTEEN

GUNPLAY

Nothing to do with the second hunt for a missing Annette Devereaux went down well with Granite Roads.

He was in a nasty disposition. Why were they tracking the woman yet again? It was infernal bad luck to have her snatched out from under their noses. He still didn't know who to blame. Sitting his mount like a thundercloud that crackled with jagged lightning, no one, not Nettie, not Brandy, not Budrow came near him. Unless he was half asleep by the campfire at night. Even then, it never seemed like a good idea.

It was not just the idea of another search for Annette that displeased him, though that was enough on its own. There was a boil festering by his instep he felt he needed to lance but was reluctant to do so for fear of infection. He had seen what infection did to men on the battlefield. Tens of thousands never made it home for no other reason.

Then there was the water. No matter where they found it, even if they discovered an underground spring they'd been told about, it was brackish. The only time he could swallow it without gagging was at dawn after the night had cooled it considerably in his canteen.

And there was the feeling that crawled about in his gut and poked its way up and down his spine. Something was brewing. Something was in the air, something was in the dust.

He'd had exactly the same feeling on a patrol in Virginia.

When the saber blow came, a mad Yankee crashing out of the woods on his mount, swinging wildly, decapitating Roads's adjutant. Roads had been half-expecting it and put a bullet clean through the bluecoat's brain, the grey matter spewing over the Yankee's back and shoulders.

Roads sensed something similar was going to occur quickly and drew two Navy Sixes, one from his holster, the other from underneath his gun belt.

The only thing that caught his attention, focused as it was like a hawk's, was a covered wagon, several hundred yards ahead. He had asked for half a dozen cowboys from the ranch, and they would be the first ones to reach it. About the time they did, Roads realized there were two wagons—he hadn't noticed one was in front of the other. For a reason he could not explain, he urged his horse into a fast trot.

The cowhands joked with the driver of the first wagon they came to, touched their hat brims in salute to a lady or ladies Roads could not see, then walked their horses further ahead.

Everything inside of Roads was screaming, though he still had no clear comprehension why. Nevertheless, his body and mind had been right in Virginia only a few years back. He kicked Sharpsburg into a gallop about the same time as he saw the back flaps get thrown aside on the wagon the cowhands were now approaching, the leader of the train. Suddenly, there were gun flashes that leaped from the darkness inside. The sharp snaps of firearms reached him a second later. He saw a cowboy fall sideways from his horse.

Then the back flaps of the wagon in front of Budrow, Brandy, and Nettie were yanked open. Roads spotted a rifle poking its snout at Brandy, and that was enough. His rebel yell came without him willing it. He fired at full speed over the heads of his friends. That's what cavalry did. That's what they were good at.

He emptied both pistols in a cloud of gray and pearl smoke. One man fell out of the wagon. Another sagged over the tailgate.

There were flames from within the wagon, and Brandy flew off her horse as if a twister had caught her.

Roads belted his empty pistols and produced a third from under his left arm. On top of the wagon now, a bullet ripped his sleeve, and another punched off his hat, but that did not stop him from emptying his third Navy Six into two women he could see aiming Henry rifles with their distinctive brass breeches. They both fell back as if slugged in the face, jerking and twitching, their Henrys firing wildly into the canvas wagon cover.

Up ahead, they shot another cowboy out of the saddle while the other two poured fire at the wagon that was blasting them.

Nettie spurred her horse past Roads to the front of the wagon that had attacked them. She fired at whoever was driving as fast as she could squeeze the trigger on her LeMat.

Nine shots later, she reached out for the harness of the left horse of the pair. The wagon swerved around, and Roads saw the bullet-punched bodies of two women in calico dresses on the driver's seat. Blood splotches and bone chips were everywhere, the women's heads smashed open. They had pistols in their laps.

"Maybe they were put up to it at gunpoint," Nettie grunted, fighting to bring the wagon team to a standstill.

"Maybe they were paid in dirty Yankee dollars. I didn't have time to ask. God can sort it out."

A shot from the other wagon missed her and dropped the horse she was reining in. Budrow roared past her towards the lead wagon.

Three of the cowhands were sprawled in the dirt. The fourth had jumped from his saddle and was firing at the wagon from behind his horse.

Budrow got close enough to use a coach gun, a sawed-off shotgun Roads didn't even know he had. There was a loud explosion as Budrow fired both barrels into the back of the wagon.

Roads marveled the Yankee could reload the coach gun as he urged his horse forward. He heard two gunshots but could not tell if they had hit Budrow. If they had, it did not stop him from firing the coach gun a second time at whoever was driving. The horses panicked and ran.

But Budrow had jumped into the driver's seat before they broke into a gallop, their nostrils flaring, their eyes rolling back white.

Roads could see it cost him a huge amount of effort, but Budrow hauled back on the reins and brought the team under control. Unbelievably, one of the drivers he'd shot gunned reared up and slashed at him with a knife.

Nettie used her Henry to cut the man clean in two. He sagged over the body of a woman. She was in a calico dress like the ones in the other wagon.

A bullet smacked into Roads's saddle. He jumped clear, expecting another round.

It came from the wagon that brought up the tail of the short train.

Brandy blasted a man with her own Navy Six from where she was on the ground, pushing herself up on one elbow. Her target fired back, clipping her right boot. Brandy's hammer clicked on an empty chamber.

Roads had no bullets left himself. He rushed his horse at the moving wagon, timed it, and leaped. He was half in and half out of the wagon bed. A bearded man in rough buckskins, astonished at Roads's sudden and clumsy arrival, brought his breech-loading rifle to bear.

One part of Roads's mind immediately identified it as an Allin Conversion, 1866, in .50 caliber. Allin was the Master Armorer of Springfield Armory in Yankee Massachusetts, and he'd figured out how to turn the old .58 caliber war muskets into modern firearms.

Another part of Roads's mind calculated that he'd fancy one of those if he survived the scrap he was in.

Yet another part of his mind remembered his knife.

All this in a heartbeat ... which he laughed about later.

Roads's hold on the wagon was precarious, and he jolted down and out of sight but for one clinging hand and one leg that straddled the tailgate. The man fired, and the bullet parted Roads's hair like a comb. He was aware there would be a second shot. Using leg, arm, and waist muscles he thought he'd left behind at Petersburg, he vaulted up and into the wagon bed while tugging his Bowie knife clear of his boot and yelling, slashing, and stabbing as if he were on a drunken rampage.

The second shot he'd expected punctured the wagon's canvas top. By that time, one of Roads's hands were crushing the bearded man's windpipe, and the other was thrusting the long blade between a pair of ribs and into the heart. The man burped up blood. He did not have long, but Roads shot a question at him anyway. "Why? I don't even know you!"

The man choked and coughed.

"And why did you drag your women folk into this assassination?" Roads pressed. "Now they are all dead."

"We're poor," the man gurgled and gasped, so that Roads scarcely understood him. "A pouch ... of silver ... was ... worth it." He was gone.

Gunfire erupted again.

Roads crawled out to the driver's seat, snatched the reins from a dead woman's hands, reined back, gritting his teeth and growling to himself, and finally brought the one horse to a standstill, the other dead and being dragged along in its harness.

A bullet ripped open his cheek. Another raked his left hand. Blood spurted into his eyes.

He could not see the man who shouted. But he recognized the voice.

"You scum buckets can't take a hint, can ya?"

It was Scat Jansen, Ricketts' right hand ugly. "Budrow? Sure, that's who we want, but the rest of you? There's no need for you all to get killed, especially the lady folk." Scat laughed. "But I reckon I'll just toss Budrow over his saddle and bring him along. Ricketts can carve him up at his leisure. I've pistol whipped him into the dust. He ain't going nowhere unless I drag him there. The rest of you ain't going nowhere either. Except to hellfire and purgatory. I'm done dancing with ya."

More gunfire. Nothing struck.

Scat hadn't sent it his way.

"Well, now, you girls, don't ya know enough to play dead? I'd a' let you be and finished off Granite there, that sorry excuse for a rebel cavalry officer. Heck, you come to the party so late you didn't make any difference at Gettysburg. No, sir, you and Jeb were dead useless. And here General Lee and the rest of us counting on ya. But here's what ya should've catched in Pennsylvania."

Roads dove off the wagon, not seeing much, and swiped at his eyes, wriggling up against the dead horse.

Stone chips stabbed his face and ricochets sang. All he had to hand was a derringer, but it gave him two shots. Scat just needed to roam closer.

Roads blinked and watered his eyes and blinked again. Finally, he could see something. Scat wasn't coming for him. He'd sent a tall, lean pitchfork of a man to do that.

Scat was heading towards Nettie and Brandy. So were two men with him.

Nettie had been hit and couldn't even sit up. It looked to Roads like her pant leg was soaked in blood. Brandy was down and not moving.

Scat stood over Nettie. "It's a pity, girl, but your long play at trying to prove you're better than a man is about to trickle out into the dirt." He pointed his pistol. "Still and all, it truly is a great pity."

There was no fancy ace for Roads to play. All he had was a deuce. And deuces weren't wild. Not this round. But you played what you were dealt. He always had.

He jumped up and fired and plugged the pitchfork man in the gut. The man bent double and dropped to his knees. Roads jumped him, jerked pitchfork's neck hard to the left, and drew the dead man's Colt.

"Leave her be, Scat!" Roads yelled. "Or I'll cut you down!"

Scat looked over at him and grinned. "I don't think so, war hero."

A blast of white sent Roads flying. An enormous man towered over him. Roads saw he'd been hammered with the butt of the man's revolver. Roads blinked, shook his head, and blinked again. Everything moved in and out of focus.

"I don't think I'll waste a good bullet," the man rumbled. "Not on Southern trash."

He dropped on Roads with all his weight, making Roads gasp, grinned, and wrapped his meaty hands around Roads's throat. He stank of garlic. "Don't worry, trash. This'll be quick. Your neck ain't no more than what God gave a scrawny chicken." His thumbs pressed hard into Roads's windpipe.

Bits of light whirled in front of Roads's eyes.

"Count to ten," the garlic man grunted. "That'll make it easier on you. You won't reach ten."

There were four or five shots. The garlic man belched and fell sideways.

Roads fought out from under the man's heavy body and went into a crouch.

Scat was still standing over Nettie, but he was facing away. The men who'd accompanied him were on their stomachs. Dark patches spread beneath both.

"I should've just put six or seven new holes in ya," Scat was hissing.

Budrow was on his feet. He threw one gun down and kept the second on Scat.

"I'm giving you another chance," Budrow replied. "Go ahead. I'm hoping for a dime novel ending to all this gunplay."

CHAPTER NINETEEN

START THE BALL

Scat Jansen raised his hands. "How do you want to do this, Budrow? Guns, knives, fists? I've waited a long time to get you pushin' up daisies."

Budrow was smiling. "Jansen, you're a lowlife, scum-sucking coyote. If I was anything like you, I'd gun you down where you stand. But I'm going to give you a chance. Put your gun back in your holster."

Jansen grinned, and the missing tooth in front made a black hole against his yellow fangs. "This is perfect. I remember you when you came to our company. A white-skinned, soft-handed easterner whose daddy got him a commission. You didn't even hardly know what a pistol was. This will be easy."

"Yeah, you're right, Jansen. I was a tenderfoot all the way. But I wasn't a tinhorn like you and your dog of a brother."

"You leave my brother out of this!"

"Why? It's because of him we're even here. Little Scat, following big brother Jimmie Lee around like a lapdog. Whatever Jimmie said, you did, including rob and rape. Your brother didn't deserve to live, and neither do you. I gave him an even break. I told him to drop his pistol, but he just didn't want to be a good soldier, did he? No, he had to try his luck. So stupid, Scat. One thing about you Jansens—you may be ugly, but you're so stupid."

The red was mounting in Jansen's face. He gave Budrow a look of pure hatred. "What do you mean, Budrow?"

"I mean, your brother tried to draw his pistol and kill me while I had the drop on him. And your stupid cousin, Ace, tried the same. Both of them dumb as a bag of rocks. After shootin' honest southern boys for a year, do you really think it wasn't easy for me to plug your brother? And then little Scat screamed like a girl and ran. Lied to the Colonel and got a false witness. But you didn't get me hanged, did you, Scat?"

Jansen's face twisted. "You was lucky back then."

Budrow's face was grim. "Let me tell you somethin', Jansen. That was then, and this is now."

Jansen squinted at Budrow. "Whaddaya mean? Today is the day I'm sendin' you to hell."

Budrow laughed and then put a sneer in his voice. "You? Why Scat, even back then, without the help of your cowardly brother and cousin, you never saw the day you could send me anywhere. I've been down the river and over the mountain since I last saw you. And I've seen you draw, Jansen. I was your captain, remember. You fancy yourself some kinda gunfighter, but you're just a wash woman. Sure, you've killed people, women and kids, mostly, but when did you ever face a real man faster than you with a pistol?"

Scat's face was bright red and twisted in hatred. "Go ahead, Budrow, put your gun away and let's do this."

Budrow laughed. "Glad to, Scat. And as for you sending me to hell, if you do, I'll be waitin' at the door for you." He slid his pistol into its holster. "I killed your brother and your cousin ... and now, I'm gonna kill you."

Incredibly fast, Jansen's hand went for his gun. Yet even with a split-second head start, he never could have beaten the blurring swift motion of Budrow's hand, the gun that sprang up. Jansen's gun muzzle was only rising when he saw the pistol aimed straight at his heart, and he knew he was dead.

He knew it with an instant of horrible recognition. In that instant, it was like there was no gap between them, and Jansen was looking straight into Budrow's blazing eyes. Then he saw the flame blossom at Budrow's gun muzzle, and he felt the bullet hit him, felt himself stagger. But he kept on drawing and then the second bullet, a lightning bolt of an instant behind the first, hit him in the hip and he started to fall. His gun finally came out. He fired, and the bullet dug up dirt at Budrow's feet. Two more shots hit him, splitting the tobacco sack tag hanging from his shirt pocket—one notched the left side and one the right. Jansen realized in that instant that he would not get even one bullet into Budrow, and he screamed as his numbing finger kept squeezing the trigger and the bullets fired wildly into the ground and then death pulled a veil over his eyes, and he was falling ... down ... down ... down into the dark.

Granite Roads rose from his crouch, shaking his head. He stared at the body of Scat Jansen as it twitched and then went still. "My word, Budrow. I never saw anything like that. When did you get faster than greased lightning?"

"Well, I had an excellent teacher, Granite. Now let's look after the girls."

Brandy opened her eyes into soft darkness. There was a fire nearby, and the light reflected off the face of the man seated beside her bedroll. His eyes were closed, and she realized that his hand enclosed hers. "Granite?"

Roads awoke with a start. He leaned over her. "Brandy? Brandy, honey." Granite's face broke into a grin. "Well, girl, it's good to see you back among the living."

Brandy looked around. "What happened?"

"You were shot, darlin', twice. Once in the shoulder and once in the side. The bullet in the shoulder went through without breaking anything, but the one in the side ricocheted off your hip bone and tore a nasty gash. You lost a lot of blood. I had to patch you up good."

"How long have I been asleep?"

"Three days, darlin'."

"Three days?" Suddenly, something occurred to Brandy, and she blushed. "When you was patchin' me up ... did you ... did you see me ... naked?"

Granite put his head back and roared. When he caught his breath, he shook his head. "No darlin'. Even when you was bleedin' like a stuck pig, you kept your honor." He laughed again.

Brandy looked around. "Where's Nettie and Budrow?"

Granite nodded toward the other side of the fire. "They're over there. Nettie took a slug in the leg, but it went through. Budrow got up from a pistol-whipping and shot Scat Jansen into blazes. I did not know the man could shoot like that."

"Well, what do you think he was doing every day away from camp? He's naturally coordinated, and after you showed him the basics, why he just kept practicing and voilá! You got yourself a real gunfighter."

Granite grinned. "Remind me not to rile that hombre. I thought I was fast, but that boy is chain lightning."

"How did our boys do?"

"Well, Brandy, we got one dead and two shot up pretty bad."

She was silent for a minute. "Who were those people who tried to bushwhack us?"

"They were a wagon train come out from Missouri. They timed it wrong and ran out of supplies several days ago. One woman was still alive. She said Ricketts waved a bag of silver money in front of their menfolk, and they agreed. Ricketts had men with guns in every wagon. He told the men he'd kill their womenfolk if they didn't go along."

Brandy was quiet. "I sure hated killing those women ..."

Granite nodded. "That's what happens in a gunfight. You shoot instinctively and feel sorry later. I shot one of my own boys at Sharpsburg. He come running through the brush from the wrong direction. Good luck for him I only winged him. And Stonewall got shot by his own troops. He was out ahead of the lines at Chancellorsville and when he rode back in the dark, some pickets challenged him. His aides yelled out who they were, but the guards didn't believe them. Thought it was a trick and shot him off his horse. He died three days later. The army was never the same."

Something occurred to Brandy. "Where's Annette?"

Granite scowled. "Ricketts, like the cowardly dog he is, seen the writin' on the wall and skedaddled outa here with the girl. I reckon they are on their way to Cloud City or Denver."

"Well, we got to find her, Granite."

"Why, for goodness' sake? I'm getting a little tired of getting shot at because of Budrow's Southern belle."

"We got to, Granite. It's me and Nettie's fault she got captured again."

"What?"

"Yeah. We were kind of, well, giving her a rough time, just joshin' her, you know. She got mad and jumped up on that big black stallion to show us she was just as much a woman as us. She spurred that black, and he lit outta there like his tail was on fire. The last we saw of her, she was headed down the road toward the gates of the ranch. Ricketts must have been lurkin' about out there, and he got her. And that's why we gotta go get her."

"Well, it's gonna be a few days before we can go. You and Nettie have to rest up. You're weak as a kitten."

"I am not!" Brandy tried to raise up, and a sharp pain shot through her side.

Seeing her grimace in pain, Granite pushed her back down. "Listen to me, girl. It's gonna be a week before we can go."

"She might be dead by then."

They heard boots coming and looked up. Budrow was standing there. "We'll go get her, but it'll just be me and Granite this time. Nettie's leg needs lookin' after. She can't ride and neither can you. We're sending you back to the ranch with the boys. Charlie will take care of you. Meanwhile, we'll ride on to Denver. If she's still alive, we'll find her."

"What does Nettie think about that."

Budrow smiled. "Well, she's not happy, but she's smart enough to know if that leg gets infected, she could lose it. So, she's going. What about you Granite?"

Roads looked up, a frown on his face.

"If you don't want to go, that's fine. I'll go alone if I

have to."

Granite stood up. "Why are you so all-fired set on saving this girl?"

"Look, I don't know if you believe in God, or Divine Providence, or the Great Spirit—whatever you want to call it. I believe God put that girl in my life for a reason, and my job won't be done until she and her daddy are safely settled in California. Our destiny is something we have nothing to say about. Somehow, even though me and Nettie will marry and raise kids on a ranch and live out our lives in the west, somehow that girl is part of the picture. It's like a call I have to answer. If you want to come with me, you're welcome."

Granite stuck out his hand. "Okay ... Kit."

Annette Devereaux lay on the bed in a small room in a cabin just outside of Denver, Colorado. It was night, and the room was dark. She had been working on the rawhide thongs that bound her wrists to the bedpost. Skin Ricketts had tied her up and then gone off to tap a whiskey barrel in the bunkhouse with his boys. He had grinned evilly when he left. "Well, Budrow and Granite are dead, so there's no reason for me to keep you around. You're just trouble. But that won't keep me from enjoying you before I kill you."

Annette looked up. "Real men protect women. I may be new to the west, but I know that when western men find out what you've done, you'll stretch a rope."

Ricketts laughed. "How will they know what I've done when your body is going to be thrown down some gully and eaten by critters? Besides, they better have ten ropes ready, 'cause I've done a lot worse. But then I guess they can only hang you once." He laughed again and turned to the man guarding the door. "Keep her quiet. Don't let her get out of there or you're a dead man."

"Yeah, well, what about sending some of that whiskey over here?"

"And have you fall asleep? Nah. I'll send someone over in a while to relieve you."

The man had grunted his assent, and they closed the door. Annette went to work right away. When Ricketts had tied her, she had twisted her wrists, so she had just a little slack, and she made good use of it. Using her strong teeth, she soon loosened the rawhide and wriggled free. Quickly, she undid her feet and then got up. The moon shone through a small window and gave her just enough light to see. She looked around. There was a chair fashioned from pieces of wood against the wall. She checked it. The thick pole that formed the headrest was loose, and she wiggled it until it came free. Then she stood beside the door and moaned. She moaned again, louder.

"Shut up in there."

"I'm sick, I need some water."

"Oh, shut up. If I come in there, you'll be sorry."

Annette groaned again, louder this time. She heard the lock click, and then, the door opened. The guard stuck his head in just far enough. With all her strength, she brought the wood piece down on the man's head. Without a sound, he tumbled into the room. Quickly, she dragged him inside the room. Then she opened the door quietly and looked around the outer room. Empty. She started to go to the door when she saw the pistol on the table.

Skin's new honcho left his new gun here. I'm going to need one.

She picked it up. It was heavy but not too heavy. The ammo belt lay beside it, so she slung it across her shoulder, crossed the room and opened the door. She could hear the men carousing in the bunkhouse. Quiet as a hunting cougar, she slipped down the porch and headed for the woods. She was free, but for how long?

CHAPTER TWENTY

Crossing the Line

Annette thought about following a creek bed into the distant mountains. There were plenty of bushes and shrubs that would render her unseen. But bears were thick, closer to the mountains, and fierce catamounts that frightened her more than the bears. And men squatted in the creek bed, as bad as the man she was trying to escape from, and she had no wish to run afoul of them. So, she made use of thickets closer to town, skirting through backyards and open lots, and headed east and south as quickly as she could, until she was within tracts of forest that had never been cleared. The woods grew darker and denser the further she traveled east and south.

She had thought to travel only by night. But her survival instincts told her that would be a mistake. Pursuers would certainly travel by day, and on horseback, and soon cut her off. They might even procure hounds to put on her trail. Annette's only hope was to sleep little, keep on going *rapido,* as the Mexicans said it, and keep changing deer trails and footpaths to throw Skin and his desperados off. She also began to make her own way through the undergrowth, hoping to leave scant sign and use routes through the trees impossible for horses to follow. Maybe stout limbs and harsh branches would knock men off their mounts or scratch their eyes out.

The problem was that where trees grew tallest and thickest was where sunlight got crowded out, which made undergrowth thin or scarce. This made it easy to walk through. But also made it easy for horses to move through too. Her best hope was to find groves of shorter trees growing up among dense stands of brush. Hard to move through but harder to track her and harder for horses.

Two days out, Annette felt sure she heard men's voices. They were far off and indistinct and probably reached her from the main path. Fear cut at her insides like a stropped Bowie. She pushed on all that day and all that night till she collapsed in a scrabble of bushes and thorns. Ignoring the way that the thorns and nettles nicked and nipped, she burrowed deep inside and fell asleep, a splinter of a waxing crescent's light on her face.

It was not dawn when she blinked awake. A man was cussing and complaining maybe a hundred yards away. She groped in her grub bag for a weapon. Annette thanked the Lord of hosts for the nagging voice that had told her to snatch up a pistol. It had taken extra time and exposed her to greater danger, but now, with Skin and his owlhoots bushwhacking for her, she took strength in the fact she could plug them with 50s, no less, and open holes big enough to drive stagecoaches through every man in the gang.

She waited, listening.

The sounds grew closer.

She steadied the pistol on her upright knees.

It was a brute of a gun.

Brand new, which was why she'd snatched it up as soon as she spied it on the table on her way out. Years before, all she'd wanted to know about was clothing, meals, and horses. Over time, unwillingly, she'd also learned a passel about guns.

This one was a fancy rig, case hardened with a floral design on the barrel and breech and had an ivory forearm and a carved ivory grip. The carving had an eagle, anchors, and the capital letters USN. The hammer and trigger guard and breechblock were gold. It was the prettiest firearm she'd ever seen, even nicer than a Henry rifle with its brass breech.

Pretty or not, Annette was past the point of waiting for others to protect her or do her killing for her. She'd cut men wide open with it if she had to. She knew it fired 50-caliber center-fire cartridges. Bat had crowed about that.

Bat Blue had become Skin's top badger since Scat had disappeared hunting down Granite Roads and Kit Budrow. Her Kit, who she prayed was safe. Bat had picked the pistol off a man he'd gunned down for the heck of it. The gun was not on the dead man's hip but in his saddle bag. Bat knew his weapons and declared it was a Remington Model 1867 Navy Rolling Block, mint, seven-inch barrel, razor accurate, perfect for taking out lawmen and other nuisances when you had the time for sniping.

She had watched him fire it a few times. He had already killed with it. Not a surprise. If anyone was more ruthless than Skin Ricketts, it was Bat Blue. Skin realized that and utilized Bat accordingly. It would just be too bad if Annette chopped him in two with the very gun Bat now prized above all others. In fact, as the sounds of men hunting her grew louder, she hoped to God that was the very thing she'd be able to do. And not just to him. To the entire gang.

Why not? Nettie Parris and Brandy Black had killed men. Why couldn't she? This wasn't Philadelphia or New

York. This was the wide-open West. Anyone could do anything here. Even her.

"I am sick to death of being afraid," she growled under her breath as she listened to branches snap, twigs pop, and horses snort. "I am sick and tired of being rescued. Today I'm going to rescue myself, Skin Ricketts. And if I get a chance to wound you, and then string you up with your own saddle rope, and watch you dance your life away at the end of it, why, sir, it shall be my pleasure. I am no longer the woman in the barn. You can darn well start being afraid of me instead of the other way around."

Annette dug some cartridges out of the ammo belt that was still around her shoulders. She set them down on the trunk of a fallen tree just beside her. A voice hollered: "This way. Over here. The tall grass is fresh trampled. We got her."

"I beg to differ," hissed Annette as she cocked the Rolling Block. "I've got you, Dirk Longmans."

He appeared on his buckskin, eyes darting left and right. He saw her. Just as she fired.

The big pistol jerked in Annette's hands and bounced off her knees. There was a roar and a gray cloud of black powder smoke. In a moment, it was gone. So was Dirk Longmans' head.

Annette felt nothing but relief and a deep satisfaction hard for her to describe. She could do to all of them what she had done to Dirk. They had it coming for what they'd done to her.

Raff Greenshields burst through the trees on his bay mare. "Raff!" Annette wanted Raff to look and see her, just like Longmans had done. Wanted him to see it was her pulling the trigger. Wanted him to know it was her vengeance that took his life and soul. Raff spotted her, looked twice, then whipped out his pistol.

"It was the looking twice that did you in, Raff," Annette whispered.

Her shot blasted him out of the saddle. The horse shrieked and ran, dragging Raff by the stirrup, ripping through saplings, and thorn bushes, and grass two feet high.

Content, Annette ejected the empty case and loaded a fresh round.

"It's the day of judgment, boys," she said as another rider appeared, looking all around him, trying to figure out where Raff and Dirk had gone and where the loud shots were coming from.

Suddenly the man glimpsed Annette and the big, black hole of her gun muzzle. He dove from his horse and sprawled behind a tall tree. It did not save him.

Roads allowed that though it was the slower route, coming into Denver through the woods and tall brush was decidedly better than riding in on the main road, exposed to all and to the gunsights of every *pistolero* that Skin Ricketts employed. Moreover, the trees provided shade from the sun, shelter from the wind, and kept down the summer dust.

If Budrow had had his way, they'd have exploded onto Denver's main street, guns blazing, mowing down every *bandito* that presented himself. Roads had reined him in, arguing that a cavalry charge would not answer for the problems they needed to resolve. For one, it would make them fine targets, fat as plums. For another, it would give Ricketts's gang fair warning and cause them to light out for destinations unknown. Did Budrow really want to track those plug-uglies all over again? Did he want to put Annette through that one more time?

"We have a pretty good idea this is where they are," Roads stated. "We can make our way into Denver slow and easy and under cover of night, draw no undue attention, find out what we need to find out, spirit Annette Devereaux to safety, then deal with the outlaws in a manner befitting their crimes. It can even be like one of those dime adventures you apparently wish to emulate. Kit Budrow, King of the Plains."

"Ha!" snorted Budrow.

"Rushing headlong into gunfire is not advisable, sir. I'd have thought you'd learned that in the past war, particularly in Virginia, at Fredericksburg. Frontal assaults are costly, and foolhardy, and rarely achieve the attackers' desired aim for launching the assault in the first place."

"Isn't that what you did on the third day at Gettysburg?"

Roads took his time in responding. He tugged a flask of brandy from a coat pocket, took a long swallow, offered it to Budrow, who shook his head, refastened the stopper, and slipped the flask out of sight. He cleared his throat.

"Now, as to the third of July 1863 in the afternoon, as I remember it ..."

The shot was loud and made both horses jolt.

"That is no 44," said Budrow.

Roads reached down to pat his horse and calm it. "No, indeed. More like a 50 or 58. Like musket fire."

Budrow pointed to the woods on their left. "There is a spurt of smoke."

"I see it."

"Perhaps someone is hunting."

"But hunting what?"

There was another shot. More smoke puffed up out of the trees. A man yelled.

"It is gunplay," Budrow said, turning his horse into the forest.

"Watch you don't ride right into it," Roads warned, but followed Budrow into the woods, one revolver already in his right hand.

There was a third gunshot. A fourth. Then a shower of sharp reports as smaller calibers got involved.

"I reckon we have ourselves a little skirmish going on here," Roads announced.

Annette had dropped into a crouch, then laid down full length behind a log, once Ricketts's men returned her fire. She was fine with that. She had decided not to retreat, and seeking cover was not a retreat.

From behind the log, she fired and opened a railway line in her fifth target, Cobb Sutton. She detested the man, detested his oily touch and odiferous breath. Now he was done and gone to make excuses to God and the devil. And she and her Iron Horse had secured the three-way discussion in eternity's parlor.

This sat well with her. The more the gunfight carried forward, the more at ease she felt. A shot from Skin Ricketts had clipped her shoulder, but the wound scarcely bled, and she was none the worse for it. Another had singed her hair and a third, courtesy of Bat Blue, notched her right ear. That stung. It had bled prodigiously for a minute or two, then coagulated straightaway. It didn't bother her. It angered her.

Annette was in a stronger frame of mind and body than she had been in months, perhaps years. Instead of thinking how she might get free of the shootout, she schemed about taking the fight to them. She was aware the gang was attempting to flank her on the left and on the right. So, she wriggled forward on her knees and elbows, extra ammo in her shirt pocket, heading back the way she had come from town, passing two outlaws she'd shot. She made a nest for herself, hunkering down and turning, aiming her Rolling Block at the log she'd lain behind for most of the gun battle, and waited.

Annette was confident the gang would attack the spot, that their heads had been down as they maneuvered in the grass and that no one had noticed her crawling away. She could not explain the sudden change in her whole being that made her eager to fight rather than flee. She supposed she had crossed a line somewhere and would not be bullied, molested, abducted, beaten, slapped, or bound with ropes and gagged. That life was over and done. Annette would not tolerate it a minute longer.

Part of her would like to have had Kit and Granite there to save her yet again. But she refused to rely on others any longer to decide her fate, whether men or women. If necessary, she would defend herself and carve her own path. Why couldn't she be the heroine of her own story? If Kit liked those dime novels, she liked them just as much or more. She enjoyed the women who fought their own fights rather than waiting for brave men to show up and set them free. In her bag, she'd kept her favorite book, dog-eared and grimy, Sal of Red Rock Canyon. Sal had done it all, including whipping men in horse races, fisticuffs, and gunfights with pistols and carbines. She'd even raised her own herd of beef cattle and founded her own ranch, beating off rustlers, owlhoots, and ne'er-do-wells, along with bears, wolf packs, and catamounts. Floods hadn't stopped her. Neither had prairie fires, blizzards, or hailstorms.

Now, as Annette waited to see what the gang would do, she wondered if Sal of Red Rock Canyon had inspired her to make her stand. Or had it been Deborah of the Book of Judges? Or Jael, who had slain an enemy general by driving a tent peg through his skull as he slept, trusting he was safe with her? She did not know. But the fear that had paralyzed her for years was gone. She had become someone else. And, as she raised her gun at a man snaking through the grass to her old hideout, she knew beyond a shadow of a doubt she was comfortable with the change.

It was Bat Blue. Perfect. She licked her lips and cocked her Remington.

Bat looked perturbed and frustrated.

Even from hundreds of feet away, she heard him cursing.

She smiled and called out, "Looking for me, Bat? I'm right here! With the pistol you stole!"

Bat jerked his head up to look.

She tightened her finger on the trigger.

Suddenly, Kit Budrow and Granite Roads came smashing through the forest on their mounts, firing shots into the air and yelling for all they were worth. Budrow waved to her while Granite peppered the woods with bullets.

"Annette! Annette!" Budrow called. "We're here! Are you all right?"

Bat Blue had vanished.

Annette lifted her head and glared at the two men, fury scribbling lines all over her face. "Carson Budrow!" she shouted. "You just ruined my shot!"

CHAPTER TWENTY-ONE

HELL ON WHEELS

"Where's Ricketts?"

Granite came off his horse to stand by Annette's hiding place. Carson rode slowly up to them.

Annette smiled demurely. "He's not here. I don't think he thought I could get away or defend myself, so he sent Bat Blue to do the job. What he didn't figure was that I've learned a few things since I came west. Especially hanging around Nettie and Brandy."

Budrow looked around at the scene. He could see the boots of one man sticking out from under some chaparral. A little way beyond that was another man, lying face down in the dirt. Since he was missing most of his head, Budrow assumed he was dead. He lifted his hat and scratched his head.

"Two dead men. I guess you have learned a few things."

"Don't forget the one behind the tree over there. He thought that big limb would save him, but it sure didn't stop this fifty from finding him."

Granite shook his head. "Well, I should smile. This is the durndest thing I've seen since my sister thought that pretty black skunk was a kitty."

Both men laughed.

Suddenly, there was a shout behind them. "Drop your guns or meet your maker."

They whirled. Bat Blue stood there, a wicked grin on his face, gun in his hand. But Annette, who was off to the side, turned slowly, the enormous gun leveled right at Blue.

"No, you skunk, you drop your gun."

Blue shook his head. He had the drop on Budrow and Roads, but Annette was out of his line of fire, and she had the bigger gun.

"Go ahead and shoot, Blue, but that bullet won't be halfway to my friends before your head comes clean off your shoulders."

Bat started to turn, but Annette called him. "Move one more inch and you'll be buzzard bait."

"Now, little missy, you won't shoot ol' Bat. Wasn't I nice to you back at the cabin?"

"Yeah, you snake, while you were undressing me with your eyes. And if you want to start something, just twitch. Now, drop your gun!"

A bead of sweat formed on Blue's face. He was in a tough spot. He had to kill the girl first, but she surely had the upper hand. "Now girlie, what do you want to shoot ol' Bat for? Let me just kill these two and then you and me will go off together, get a little ranch somewhere. Why, with a woman like you, I could be somebody."

Annette laughed. "I'd sooner crawl into a hog pen and lay in the slop than go anywhere with you, you murdering sidewinder."

The blood rose in Bat's face, and he choked out his words. "I'm not scared of you, you're just a girl. You couldn't hit me if you tried."

"Yeah? Well, tell that to Dirk Longman and his sidekick, Raff. Now drop your gun, you yellow dog."

Bat's face flushed with blood. Forgetting Kit and Granite, he whirled on his tormentor. But before he could get his barrel around to draw down on Annette, the big gun flashed fire and boomed. A bright red flower bloomed on the front of Bat's shirt. He went to his knees. His gun went off at the impact, and the bullet clipped off a lock of Annette's hair. The gun in her hand belched fire again and knocked Bat backwards into a heap. He twitched as his gun dropped into the dirt. Annette walked over and stood above the outlaw. He stared up at her with unbelieving eyes.

"Goodbye, Bat. When you see your partners in hell, be sure and tell them it was a slip of a Southern belle that shot you down like the mangy cur you are."

He choked out his last words. "You ... you ..." Bat's eyes closed—he was dead.

The three riders rode into Cloud City—two lean, tough-looking cowboys and a beautiful girl dressed in men's clothes, a flat-brimmed hat pulled low over her eyes and a big pistol slung around her hips. They rode down the street to the marshal's office. Budrow dismounted. A man wearing a marshal's star was asleep in a chair that was leaning against the wall. He was old, and he wore no gun. His striped suspenders stretched over a fat belly that lopped over his belt, and his gray hair was greasy and long.

Budrow spoke. "Marshal?"

The old man opened one eye and looked up at Budrow. "Whaddaya want?"

"Ricketts."

The old man opened both eyes and looked at Budrow, then at Granite and Annette. "Don't know him." He closed his eyes again.

Budrow hooked his boot under the leg of the chair and pulled. The marshal went over backwards, banging his head as he hit the boardwalk in a heap. "What the devil ..." He scrambled up. Budrow helped him by grabbing his shirt front and pulling him to his feet.

"Now, Marshall, where's Ricketts?"

The old man squirmed in Budrow's grasp. Budrow lifted his hand.

"All right, all right. He's down at the Silver Dollar ..." He squinted at Budrow. "You Roads?"

Budrow jerked his head back at his silent partner. "That's Roads, I'm Budrow."

The old man cackled. "Yeah, wal, Skin knows you is comin'. I wouldn't give you a snowball's chance in hell of getting outta this town."

Budrow pulled him closer. "If you're the marshal, where's your gun?"

The old man gulped and looked around. "Skin won't gimme one."

Budrow reached down and tore the star off the man's chest. "Any man who wears this star should stand up for the folks in his town, not let some two-bit Comanchero run him around the flagpole. Now here's my offer. Go down to the livery, get your horse and head south or east or west, because after we finish with Ricketts, if we see you, we'll kill you."

The old man turned white and put up his hands. "Okay, okay, I'm going."

Budrow shoved him aside, and the old man stumbled into the street. He turned and pointed a boney finger at the trio. "We'll see who does the killin'. Haw, haw." He headed off down the street.

Budrow turned to Roads. "If Ricketts knows we're coming, he'll try to box us. Do you know this town?"

Granite nodded. "Yeah, been here a few times. The Silver Dollar is just down the street. There's an alleyway between it and the bank, and across the way is the livery stable. Ricketts will have a rifleman in the hayloft and a couple of men in the alley. When I call him out, he'll come out, but he'll be depending on his men to get me first. That's why you have to be in the livery stable."

"When you call him out?"

"Yep. You got Jansen, Ricketts is mine. I got a long score to settle with that owlhoot. He killed my best friend when he was only sixteen."

Budrow saw the set to Granite's jaw and knew that arguing would do no good. "Okay, you got him. I'll take the man in the livery. But what about the alleyway?"

"I'll have to take my chances."

Annette coughed. "That's what I dislike about men. They think they are the only ones who can do the shooting."

Granite looked up at Annette. She was not the same girl they rescued from Skin the first time. Her weeks with Nettie and Brandy while they were fetching Charlie's cattle up from New Mexico had stood her in good stead.

"Well, girl, you've changed."

Annette slipped down off her horse. "My daddy taught me to shoot and ride when I was a little girl. It was my mama who dressed me in silks and satins and made me drink tea. But that's not who I really am. Being with Nettie and Brandy showed me that a woman can be powerful and feminine too. It seems to me you western men need western women cut from the same cloth. If you remember, Budrow, when you found me in the stable with Jansen and his brother, they were going to pay a price to get to me."

Budrow remembered all right. The beautiful Annette, with her torn dress down around her waist, backed against a wall with a razor-sharp pitchfork in her hands and the Jansen brothers trying to figure out what to do next.

"Yes, ma'am, I remember."

"You killed them, but I would have got at least one of them on my own. And by the way, since Bat had the drop on you, and I pulled your tail out of that mess, I figure we're even. Now what's my part in this fandango?"

Budrow and Roads looked at each other and grinned. Granite pointed toward the alleyway. "Trees border the town behind the buildings on both sides. Annette, you slip down and get set up behind the cottonwoods by the saloon. When those boys come out the back door, they'll be concentrating on the street. You just injun' up behind 'em and get the drop on them when the ball starts. Ricketts will yell for his men to get me. When he does, start the dance. Okay, let's do it."

Budrow headed around the marshal's office and worked his way silently toward the livery stable. Annette crossed the street and disappeared behind the bank. Granite checked the chambers of both his guns, spun the cylinders and slipped them into the tied-down holsters. He stretched his arms, pulled his hat down to keep the sun out of his eyes, and started up the street.

Budrow came to the back door of the livery stable. It was standing open. He slipped inside. It was cool, and there was a pleasant barn-like smell of hay, manure, and horses. A horse stomped in a stall and blew contentedly through his nose. Budrow slipped down the row of stalls, the horses rolling the whites of their eyes at him as he passed. He came to the ladder that led up to the loft. He stopped and listened. Above him was silence and then ... a slight sound. Budrow tried to see up through the cracks. Up above, by the loft door, a drift of dust sifted down. Silently Budrow climbed the ladder. Granite had been right. There was a man with a Winchester, waiting to gun down Granite as soon as the shooting started. Budrow eased his head up and lifted his gun over the edge of the floor. Then he waited.

Annette slipped behind the bank and into the trees. She made her way quietly down until she was concealed in the brush at the end of the alleyway. The back door of the saloon creaked open, and two men came out, pistols in their hands. Annette lifted her big fifty and waited.

Granite came down the street. The air was still. The dust beneath his feet stirred in little puffs. The tall cottonwoods behind the saloon brushed their polished leaves together, but there was no other sound. Granite dried his sun-browned hands on his jeans. His face was still and cold, like a block of carved stone. He pulled his hat brim a little lower and put his hands on his gun butts, loosening them in the holsters. Then he smiled and called out.

"RICKETTS!"

There was a moment of silence, the double doors into the saloon swung open, and Skin Ricketts stepped into the light. The scar across his chin that ran up to his ear was red against his pale skin. He wore two guns, like Roads. He grinned.

"Well, well. Granite Roads. Been expecting you, boy."

"Hello, Ricketts. Been a long time since you gunned down my friend. But that was easy for you since he was unarmed. And maybe you didn't notice, but I ain't the boy you pistol-whipped and left for dead."

Granite could see Rickett's jaw tighten. He went on.

"You've always been a coward, Ricketts, ever since those days back on the Canadian. You get men to kill for you, but you never take any chances on your own."

"What do you mean?"

"Like the bushwhacker you got up in the loft over there, and the two coyotes skulking in the alleyway. You think you got me boxed."

Ricketts grinned again. "I do ..." But there was hesitation in his voice. "Say, where's that partner of yours?"

"Oh, he's handy."

"You don't stand a chance."

"C'mon, Ricketts. If you want to do this, let's go. Otherwise, drop your guns and we'll hang you up in that cottonwood down the street."

Ricketts looked around, uncertainty on his face. Then he opened his mouth and hollered, "TAKE HIM!!

When Ricketts hollered, two things happened. Budrow slapped the floor with his left hand. The man in the loft window turned at the sound. Seeing Budrow, he lifted his rifle, but Budrow was quicker. Two shots blazed out and two bursts of red opened on both sides of the rifleman's top shirt button. The man looked surprised, coughed, and dropped his rifle. Then he toppled backwards out of the loft and crashed down onto the street below.

At the same time, the two men in the alley stepped forward. They didn't expect a woman's voice.

"Howdy, boys."

They both turned and saw something else they didn't expect. A she-wolf with a big 50-caliber pistol. "Drop 'em or die," came the order. One man, dumber than the other, raised his gun. The result was instantaneous. The end of Annette's gun blossomed fire, and the first man blew backwards against the wall of the saloon like he'd been roped off a running horse. His dying fingers squeezed the trigger, but his bullet dug a furrow in the dirt at Annette's feet. The second man dropped his pistol and raised his hands. "I'm out of it, I ain't shooting."

"Down on your face."

The man dropped obediently. There was a sound, and Annette saw a man with a bartender's apron coming out the back door. He had a shotgun and brought it down on Annette, but before he could level it, he took two bullets in the stomach. The shotgun blasted a hole in the steps as the man tumbled face down into the dirt.

Out in the street, Skin Ricketts watched as his bushwhacker fell out of the loft. He heard two shots and then a third mixed with the roar of a shotgun. Then there was silence.

From out of the alley came Annette's voice. "Okay back here, Roads."

Kit Budrow stepped to the loft entrance. "Good here."

Granite looked back at Ricketts. "Okay, Ricketts, make your play."

Ricketts looked around desperately.

"Nobody's coming, Skin. It's time to pay the piper."

Frantically, Ricketts clawed for his gun. It hadn't even cleared leather when Road's first shot took him in the throat. He struggled to lift the gun, but it seemed to fire on its own. The second shot took him chest high, and the third drilled a neat hole between his eyes. Skin Ricketts stared in amazement, Granite Roads saw the light pass from his eyes, and he toppled face forward into the dust.

CHAPTER TWENTY-TWO

SAL OF RED ROCK CANYON

"Tell me how you'd write it! Please!"

"My lady, I must think on it. I will need a decent cigar, some brandy or cognac, if cognac is possible. A moment to myself."

"Do you truly want a moment to yourself?"

"Right now, I confess, I do not."

"Mmm. So, Granite, the war hero, likes to dance with me?"

"I do indeed, Miss Devereaux."

"And what would Brandy think of that?"

"Why, nothing much at all, provided I danced with her as well. We are not married, Miss Devereaux, nor is there an engagement in the near future."

"But you are fond of one another."

"Indeed, we are."

"Well, never mind all that. Tell me how you'd write my dime novel, Granite."

He swept her about the dance floor of fresh sawn planks, bright with candles from a simple chandelier overhead. Three other couples waltzed around them. Two violins provided the music, that was all, but Annette found them more than adequate for an enjoyable, romantic evening.

She had proven she was as tough as Nettie Parris or Brandy Black when it came to gunplay and defending herself. Now she was going to prove to Granite and Kit she could be a lady as well. One that could turn their heads. She was grateful the other two women were not there. It gave her free rein.

Granite told her how he would write up her adventure with the outlaws. She smiled at his boyish eagerness and laid her head gently on his chest, on the white shirt. One of his hands held hers and another was upon the silky material of the dress she wore, one that draped wonderfully over her body and shimmered as they moved smoothly to the violins.

There had been reward money from the sheriff in Denver for the death or apprehension of Skin Ricketts and his gang. Even though she had protested valiantly, Granite and Kit had given the entire sum to her. "You've gone through enough," Budrow had told her. "And you wiped out half the gang on your own. You deserve it, Annette."

So, after a suitable amount of protest, she had taken the money and bought herself such finery as Denver could offer. She knew she looked like a belle in her dress, shoes, and beautifully styled hair. Men stopped in their tracks on the street, which pleased her. She had been scruffy and ignored long enough. Now she wanted to be considered akin to a princess.

That Granite had cottoned to her was a bonus. Three days in Denver had accomplished that. She had not expected it. But she luxuriated in his attention, making sure he was well aware she enjoyed his Texas charm, and intended to make good use of it. She slipped a peek at Kit Budrow. He was standing at the edge of the dance floor, looking lost and confused, hands in his pockets. Good. Let him remain lost and confused. She wanted him to stay in that state until he grew desperate for her.

THE DRIVE

I need handsome Kit Budrow absolutely besotted.

Looking at herself in the mirror in her room in Denver, she had been concerned. There had been so many rough and tumble years, she wondered if she had lost any ability she may have had to tangle up a man's thinking or place a strain and weight on his heart. But after only a day, she realized she had nothing to worry about. Granite was eating out of the palm of her hand. This tickled her fancy and pleased her immensely. With a little extra work, Annette was confident Kit would fall headlong into the lovely snare she had set for him.

The woman at the shop had said she looked bewitching in the new dress, with her shining dark hair pinned up. Annette had silently agreed and thanked her. She gloried in the moment. Shy until her gunfight with Skin Ricketts' gang had birthed another spirit in her breast, she found she now held to a new confidence in every conceivable area of her life. Purchasing several dresses, blouses, and skirts, her skin and face clean and smooth and bright, she knew she sparkled like the sun, like the stars, like a gemstone. When men's eyes lingered, she was not offended. She craved to be noticed and become the stuff of their hopes and dreams. She had been shoved to the corner long enough.

"I like your ideas, Granite." She had not been listening. It was enough he took the writing of a dime novel in her honor so seriously he was mapping it out in his head. What mattered now was that they continue to waltz under the chandelier, and she savor Kit turning absolutely green with envy, and alternately, scarlet with jealousy. Her smile on her perfectly touched up lips grew as Kit's discomfort on the sidelines increased, and he began to pace.

Annette giggled into Granite's shirt. Big, strong Kit Budrow was tumbling helplessly into a love for her as big as the Rocky Mountains. Things couldn't be turning out better. She was ecstatic about her life. To let it sink into Kit's heart even deeper, and sting that much sharper, Annette asked Granite for a fifth dance and felt a wonderful surge of delight when he eagerly said yes. He was twisted around one of her little fingers, Kit around the other. Never mind being a princess. She felt like an all-powerful queen.

I can get whatever I want from them. A far cry from three months ago. God, thank you, thank you. Please don't let up.

"If I may say," Granite whispered in her ear, pausing in his headlong discourse about how he'd write up Annette's dime western, "you truly have blossomed since you set those outlaws dead to rights. It is an astonishing transformation. I think of a delicate blossom, pounded down by a heavy rain, drooping. Then it shakes the water off, springs upright, and is more lustrous and beautiful than before."

"Oh, Granite, that is the sweetest thing to say to me." Despite the game she was playing, Annette was genuinely touched. "Do I honestly look as splendid as you say I do?"

"Even more so. There are no words. You have come from darkness into the light of day."

"You are too kind, sir."

She pecked him on the cheek. She could see he liked it. But although the kiss was delivered to him and left its crimson mark, she intended it for Kit Budrow. She was confident it would make him squirm. A quick glance confirmed her hopes. Kit looked as if someone had skewered him. Wonderful. She continued waltzing with Granite.

"One more dance, please, sir."

"You are insatiable, Miss Devereaux."

"After all my years under a shroud, I expect I am, Mr. Roads."

"You mean to make up for lost time?"

"I do."

"You are well on your way."

"Splendid. That's gallant of you."

Annette thought of leaving her mark on his cheek again but did not want Kit's locomotive to run off the rails. She was confident he had built up a full head of steam—or rather, she had built it up in him—and did not want his boiler to burst. What if he challenged Granite to a duel? She knew she had a lot to learn and relearn about being a lady, but one thing was certain in her mind—men could be fools over women. She wanted the two men to be dazzled over her transformation. She did not want them to kill each other over it.

They finished their seventh dance. Annette said she needed to freshen up, while Granite claimed he required a bourbon from the bar. She did not meet Kit Budrow's parched gaze as she glided past in her shimmering dress. Let his tongue hang down to his boots. This was a gunfight. It was her or Nettie Parris.

The plan was to attend church on Sunday, something she had dearly missed, and the next day make their way back to the ranch and bring up the cattle to Denver. That was the overall plan. Her immediate plan was to lasso and hogtie Kit Budrow and slip him into the pocket of her riding skirt so that he was utterly and completely hers. Someone Nettie Parris could never fasten her claws into again.

Annette knew that if it came down to it, she would physically fight Nettie for Kit. Fists, kicks, throwing Nettie into the mud and pinning her, whatever it took to win. There was no question in Annette Devereaux's mind. She permitted herself the devil's smile as she looked in the restroom mirror and patted her face dry. That's how much she had changed. This was no fleeting hope. She was confident she could whip Nettie Parris with one hand. Convinced she was the stronger one now.

"Two handsome beaus," a woman at her side said. "How do you manage it?"

Annette glance at her. Trim, elegant, sure of herself.

"Oh, ma'am, it is quite manageable."

"You have them eating out of your hand."

Annette laughed, still touching herself up in the mirror. "That's the general idea, isn't it?"

"I find you too bold, too sly. I've been watching you toy with them. Those poor men are being taken on a wild coach ride."

Annette laughed again. It was a deep, dark, husky laugh. "Those poor men love it, deary."

"Don't deary me."

"Why, do you suppose you can take me on?" Annette faced her, one hand on her hip. "You'd last ten seconds against me. Perhaps only five."

The woman's face colored. "I am not some barroom brawler or whiskey-drinking cowgirl. I'm a lady."

Annette, who towered over her, flicked a piece of lint off the woman's dress. "So am I. One who survived and now is bold as brass and taking on more beautiful brass every day."

She emerged from the restroom, linked her arm through Kit's before Granite could approach them, and guided him onto the dance floor. "Your turn to tell me how you'd write my adventure story."

Annette could not miss how grateful he was to be taken into her arms. She placed her lips on his cheek a moment to secure his enthrallment, then rested her head over his heart. She listened to it pounding away. Wasn't it speeding up? She held him closer. She had him. She knew it.

"Why, I'd begin with you back east," he told her. "You would start your hunt for the men who had dishonored you there. Your quest would be relentless. Blizzards, prairie fires, and Indian attacks would not stop you, nor alkaline watering holes, buffalo stampedes, or the baking sun. Your expertise with pistol and rife would be the news of the western towns. Your reputation for beauty, deadliness, and a fast draw would go before you. Just like your heroine Sal of Red Rock Canyon, you would sweep all obstacles before you like a biblical flood. There would be no reining you in. At the very end, you would gun the desperadoes down, pocket the not insubstantial reward money, and lay the groundwork for your immense cattle ranch in Colorado."

"Mmm." Annette purred into his white shirt and chest and listened to Kit's heart work hard. "I like it. Come outside. Tell me more."

She drew him into the warm summer night.

Granite hovered by the open door, smoking a cigar and sipping his bourbon. Annette was glad he was under her thumb too. It would make it easier for her to get her way and move Nettie and Brandy out of the picture. However, right now, she needed Kit completely to herself. She took his hand and tugged him around the corner of the building. There were just a few horses hitched to a post and a lot of stars over their heads. The music of the violins reached them through an open window.

Annette watched Kit drink in her beauty and smiled in the most inviting way she could, lacing her arms about his neck. She knew she had never looked better in her life. Against all odds, she hadn't died. She hadn't been shot, and here she was, alone with the one man on earth she wanted most of all, and it was clear to her, and so wonderful, that he wanted her just as much. Who knew that standing up to what she feared would make her the woman she'd always wanted to be? Such a complete woman, such a strong woman, a woman who could hold her own against anyone, a woman who could sweep a man like Kit Budrow off his feet?

He was entranced. She kept him there, knowing starlight glistened in her big, dark eyes, knowing she was irresistible. She smiled, watching him try to fight it, knowing he couldn't win, not against what she brought to the table. Finally, he broke, like a dike bursting, caught her up in a kind of frenzy, as if he might lose her, and closed his mouth over hers, kissing her with all the strength in his body. The Annette Devereaux she had become kissed him back with all her strength too, and it was more than he expected.

Kit opened himself to her in a way he'd never opened himself to any woman, ever. He collapsed against her, spent, though she drew enough out of him to keep the kiss going a good while longer. She held him up, gripping him fiercely and with all kinds of love in her arms. This was an Annette Devereaux who could steal his soul, never mind his heart.

You're mine, Kit Budrow. Every bit of you. Every drop, every smile, every dream. Completely mine.

Granite Roads had wandered around the building from another door and finally came upon them, kissing passionately, as if they had only seconds to live, utterly oblivious of the moon, stars, and Denver, Colorado. He took a puff of his cigar, a sip of his bourbon, and chuckled to himself as he turned away.

"This is going to prove interesting. Almighty interesting."

EPILOGUE

A sundown, somewhere in the wild lands between Denver, Colorado, and the Apishapa range in 1867. Pale pink and purple streaks reach from beyond the horizon into the slowly approaching indigo of night. The last golden rays of a departing sun paint the top rim of a lonely butte at the head of the canyon with brushstrokes of light. Night birds begin their quiet songs, joining a lonely coyote in the chorus that usually brings rest to a rider's heart.

Two men sit by the fire. A pot of coffee bubbles at the edge of the fire circle as Carson Budrow builds a smoke. His trail partner, Granite Roads, takes a long cigar from his mouth and shakes his head.

"Son, you are in a terrible fix."

"You don't have to tell me, Roads. I'm the one that's in it, not you. I don't know what to do. I have to make a choice here, and it's tearing me up."

Granite Roads chuckled. "Well, I saw you kissin' the be-yootiful Annette, and it looked like you already did. Make your choice, that is."

"Roads, you know, and I know she trapped me. She … she was … I don't know … a primal woman that night. That dress, the hair, the white shoulders in the moonlight, the sweet lips, the eyes …"

"Whoa, Kit, you're getting yourself all worked up again."

"She tricked me and trapped me. She danced with you until I was crazy then led me like a lamb to the slaughter. Any man would have broken under the weight of that setup. You would have, given the chance."

Roads nodded. "I must admit, if she had let me kiss her, I would've thrown Brandy over in a heartbeat."

They smoked in silence for a while.

Budrow broke it. "What do you think I should do?"

Roads chuckled again. "No sir! You won't get me to track down that trail, no sir."

"Okay, just put yourself in my place. I have two of the most beautiful women I've ever seen after me. Annette knows I'm promised to Nettie, but that doesn't seem to bother her. I love Nettie with all my heart—over the moon—but Annette has gotten to me."

Budrow stood up and looked up at the rising moon. He took off his hat and spoke in an oratorical tone. "O what a rogue and peasant slave am I! Is it not monstrous that this player here, but in a fiction, in a dream of passion, could force his soul to his own conceit, that from her working, all his visage wann'd, tears in his eyes, distraction in's aspect, a broken voice, and his whole function suiting with forms to his conceit? All for nothing! For Hecuba!"

Granite looked at him in amazement. "Those are some might fancy words, Budrow. But what in blazes do they mean?"

Budrow sat back down. "It's Shakespeare, from Hamlet. Hamlet is calling himself out for being a deceitful fellow, a liar who could make himself weep, effect a broken voice, or whatever was necessary for the situation he was imagining. That's me, a deceitful fellow. I imagine I'm in love with Nettie, and then with Annette, then back with Nettie. I'm about to go loco."

"Who is Hecuba?"

"That's the woman Hamlet was crying for, and yet she'd been dead a thousand years. Hamlet was a phony, and so am I. I just need to get on my horse and ride west to California, get me a placer claim, live in a dugout, and let those girls go back to their lives and ..."

Granite took a sip of coffee. "Spoken like a true Yankee coward."

Budrow jumped up, hand on his pistol. "You take that back or make your play."

Granite just looked up and shook his head. "A little high-strung, aren't we?"

"Well, I'm not a coward. I'm just confused."

"Sit down, Budrow, and collect yourself." Budrow sat back down.

Roads took a long pull on the cigar. "Maybe you should take yourself a little time on your own. You got Annette waitin' in Denver and Nettie at Apishaba. Tell you what. Why don't you ride with me to Texas? I got a minor problem of my own."

"What's that?"

"You remember my sister Alice's no-good husband, Joby?"

"Yeah."

"Well, Joby and Alice finally split, and Joby took to the outlaw trail. He's been ridin' with some tough hombres. Some of them are Comancheros. I got a letter from Alice. Seems the leader of the gang wants to make the ranch their headquarters. Alice won't have none of it. She wants me to come down and help her straighten Joby and his owlhoot partners out, which I will be more than glad to do. But the odds are a little stacked against me. I could use a good hand with a gun to ride with me."

"What about the girls?"

"Well, Nettie is still recuperating from the bullet wounds she got, and so is Brandy. They can't go anywhere.

And Annette has brought her dad up to Denver and they are looking for a ranch to buy with the reward money she got. Plus, I expect old man Devereaux has got some salted away, so they'll be *occupado* for a while, sortin' all that out."

"Yeah, I'm listening."

"Well, we'll just drop the ladies a note and mosey on down Texas way for a while. Shouldn't take us longer that a month or so to get it handled. That should give you time to get yourself straightened out. And after that, well, who knows. There is a lot of country in the West. I hear there's some pretty nice territory—the mountains of New Mexico, the Tonto Basin in Arizona, Idaho, Oregon. Plenty of places that might need a couple of old soldiers to help them get civilized. What say you?"

Budrow sighed. "You're a true friend, Granite. I knew you'd come up with something."

"We'll head south in the morning then?"

"Texas it is."

And that's another story.

ABOUT THE AUTHORS

MURRAY PURA

Murray Pura has over twenty-four novels to his credit and, in addition, has published dozens of short stories, novellas and poems along with numerous books of nonfiction. He has worked with Elk Lake Publishing, Harlequin, HarperCollins, Harper One, Baker, Barbour, Zondervan, Harvest House and MillerWords, His fiction has been shortlisted for a number of literary prizes including, most recently, the Selah. Pura has lived in the UK, the Middle East, the USA and Canada. He now makes his home by the Montana border in the Rocky Mountains of Alberta. His most recent publications with Elk Lake include the stories "Black Sand" and the award-winning "Lone Star," the romance, *The Light at St. Silvan's*, and his contributions to the anthologies *The Amish Menorah*

(2020), *The Men of Amish Fiction Christmas Collection* (2020) and *Christmas From the Heart* (Christmas 2021).

PATRICK E. CRAIG

Patrick E. Craig has been a lifelong musician and writer. In 1984, he left his old life behind to follow Christ. Since then, he has been a worship leader, a pastor, a speaker, a teacher of the Word, a writer, and a published author. He has worked with Harvest House Publishing, Harlequin Publishing, Elk Lake Publishing, and has been represented by the Steve Laube Agency.

Patrick was part of a Selah Award-winning anthology for Elk Lake and a Chanticleer International Book Award semi-finalist. He also publishes unter his two imprints, P&J Publishing and Islands Publishing.

ELK LAKE BOOKS BY MURRAY PURA AND PATRICK E. CRAIG

ANTHOLOGIES
- *The Amish Menorah and other Stories* (The Men of Amish Fiction)
- *A Christmas Collection* (The Men of Amish Fiction)
- *Christmas from the Heart* (Elk Lake Authors Christmas Romances)

PURA & CRAIG
- *Beyond the Red Hills*

PURA
- "Uzura Seki—Black Sands", a Short Story
- *The Light at St. Silvans*

CRAIG
- The Adventures of Punkin and Boo:
  - *The Mystery of Ghost Dancer Ranch*
  - *The Lost Coast*